Anthony Holt MBE was a pilot and seaman officer in the Royal Navy for over 30 years, after which he began a second career running two of London's larger 'Gentlemen's Clubs' for nearly eighteen years.

He is married and lives in Dorset where he now spends his time writing, sailing and working as a volunteer Coast Watcher.

Nine Stories

of the Sea

Anthony Holt

Copyright 2014

Anthony Holt

ISBN: 978-1-291-95778-5

Disclosure

'Tui Lau' is an accurate account of the dramatic events which took place on the outer edge of the Fijian Islands in the South Pacific in 1968. It was sheer chance that placed a British warship carrying the only helicopter in that part of the ocean at the same time as a small ship ran hard aground on a reef in a rising gale. Without the intervention of the helicopter it is unlikely that many of the one hundred passengers and crew of the *Tui Lau* could have survived. I was proud to be one of the four men who saved their lives.

'A Matter of Conscience' is based upon a specific and tragic sequence of events which took place during a deployment to the United States, but some of the names and circumstances have been changed.

'Hurricane' is an account of a great storm that did take place in the middle of the Atlantic Ocean. It caused considerable damage to the two warships that it engulfed and it was only by steady, sound seamanship and the solid construction of the ships that they were enabled to emerge from the storm.

'Mutiny' is a work of fiction but put together using various incidents which did take place separately at various times. The causes of the mutiny and the immediate reactions are sadly typical of unrest which has taken place occasionally but infrequently in the ships of the Royal Navy.

'The King and I' and 'Collision' are accurate accounts of unusual events which took place onboard a Battle Class destroyer in the early 1960s. 'Dunsley Wyke' provides a brief snapshot of the demanding life aboard a clapped-out, elderly, but still operational trawler while taking passage to join the destroyer – somewhere north of Iceland.

'The Chase' connects several odd events which occurred around attempts to bring a frigate out of a major refit during the Cold War and 'Out to Lunch' is an accurate account of an amusing set of circumstances onboard Britain's fastest ever warship.

In putting these stories together I have tried to be as accurate and complete as possible and no criticism is directed towards any individual or organisation. Where I have given an opinion it is an honest opinion drawn from the information and evidence available to me at the time. If the passage of time has introduced any error then I can only apologise.

Acknowledgements

In writing my books I am indebted to my wife Irene, for her constant support and her patience towards me when things have not gone as I had expected.

Dedication

This work is dedicated to the men of the Royal Navy who served through the difficult years of the Cold War.

Contents

Tui Lau

A Matter of Conscience

Hurricane

Mutiny

The King and I

Collision

Dunsley Wyke

The Chase

Out to Lunch

Tui Lau

At just over 1200 tons, the *Tui Lau* provided a vital service through the Fijian archipelago by carrying people, stores, food and animals from the outer islands into the capital, Suva, on the main island of Viti Levu, or occasionally to various ports on Vanua Levu, the island which dominated the Northern Division.

The ship had started life as an inter-island ferry, servicing the remote communities dotted around the Baltic coast of Norway and occasionally visiting the fjords along the Atlantic coast. With the ship not yet ten years old, the Norwegian Transport and Shipping Department had decided to replace the vessel with a bigger ro-ro ship. The smaller passenger ferry had been put up for disposal. Initially there was little interest but the community leaders in the Lau islands at the edge of the Fijian archipelago had spotted the ship for sale and identified her as a possible means of linking them to the big islands dominating the South Pacific island state. A huge savings project was begun and eventually the Lau islanders were able to take possession of their own ship, at a knock-down price. She was renamed *Tui Lau* and immediately became busy servicing the Lau islands as well as carting opportunity cargoes around the other islands from time to time.

Tui Lau had a crew of nine men; and on the night of 25th October she was heading for Suva with deck cargo of crated chickens and ducks, tethered pigs and goats, timber, and an assortment of damaged machinery from a sawmill in urgent need of replacement. Additionally, she was carrying ninety-three passengers, many of them children returning to school on the main island, but including four individuals travelling separately and each visiting Fiji as part of a world tour.

Nobody knew precisely what happened to lead to the destruction of the little ship but as she approached Suva from the south-east she strayed from her plotted course. She had been due to pass to the south of the almost uninhabited island of Totoya but her actual track took her some fifteen degrees further to the east. In the days before mariners were able to rely on the accuracy of the Global Positioning System, and with the absence of systems such as Decca and Loran from the South Pacific, open ocean navigation depended upon sextant observations of the sun, moon and stars, supported by radar, careful 'dead reckoning' plots and precise steering. If the visibility remained good during daylight, visual fixes could be achieved from various islands along the route; but these might sometimes be uncertain.

During the night the wind had blown up into a full south-westerly gale and this, together with an intermittent current from the south-west, might have pushed the *Tui Lau* to starboard of her intended track. Her course was probably set to pass between Totoya Island and the equally tiny Matuka Island, about eighteen miles to the south-west of Totoya. Another possibility was that *Tui Lau's* Officer of the Watch might have confused Totoya Island with Moali to the north. Although the little ship had radar, it was well known that identifying low-lying islands from a small rolling ship with its radar aerial not far above the sea could be difficult.

Whatever the reason, *Tui Lau* veered away from her correct track, failed to see the pounding surf on the reef surrounding Totoya, and ran square onto the coral at almost full speed.

****

HMS Fife was one of the latest and most powerful vessels in the Royal Navy – as well as one of the fastest. She was designated as a guided missile destroyer, but at over six thousand tons she was more of a light cruiser. Powered by a combination of steam turbines and gas turbines, she could wind her speed up quickly to more than thirty-two knots. It was this sudden increase in speed that must first have woken me.

Fife was on her way north, with everyone relaxing after a hectic and entertaining two weeks in New Zealand. With plenty of time to reach the next port of call – Suva in Fiji – she had been rolling gently along at about twelve knots. I had turned in early and before sleep arrived I had been savouring the prospect of a quiet Saturday to follow. There was no flying planned and the only thing likely to disturb my day would be helping to clean the ship's big Wessex helicopter later that afternoon. There is a tradition in the Fleet Air Arm that the aircrew should help the maintenance crew to clean their aircraft; and as one of the two pilots on board, that included me.

The ship had been promised a traditional Saturday at sea – an afternoon off – known as a 'make and mend' in the Royal Navy. So I had been thinking of a leisurely breakfast, a bit of tidying up and an afternoon lying under the gentle South Pacific sunshine with a good book – except for the aircraft cleaning, that is.

I was still half asleep but puzzling over what had caused me to wake, and wondering why the usual vibrations of the ship that accompanied progress through the sea had risen to become urgent and persistent, when there came an authoritative rap on my cabin door. The door was immediately slid back to reveal

Leading Aircrewman 'Billy' Walker, our tough and endlessly resourceful fourth member of the helicopter crew.

"Briefing, sir, ten minutes – on the bridge."

"What did you say?"

"Briefing in ten minutes on the bridge – sir." With that he was gone and the door slammed shut. I wondered for a moment whether I was to be the victim of an elaborate joke but then, for the first time, I looked at my watch. It was 3.30 a.m. I tumbled out of bed, scratched myself, clambered into my flying overalls and boots and then stepped out into the passageway. There was more activity than was reasonable for that hour of the morning so whatever had disturbed me had disturbed others and therefore I thought it must be serious.

Clutching my blue canvas navigation bag, crammed with its load of maps, torch, knee-pad and the other paraphernalia that an anti-submarine pilot accumulates, I stumbled along towards the bridge.

When I arrived on the bridge I was told to go immediately to the Operations Room, one deck below. A change of plan already. "How unusual," I thought.

Three minutes later found me entering the Operations Room. A group had formed around the main plotting table and I recognised the ship's Navigating Officer and the Operations Officer through the dim red lighting to which my eyes were slowly adjusting. Beyond them stood my Boss, who was the other pilot in the Flight. Our Observer had maps and charts spread across the table and he was fiddling with a navigational calculator – not electronic but rather like a circular slide rule festooned with various helpful attachments.

A tall, stooping figure detached itself from a group on the other side of the room and walked across. It was our Captain who was, in my humble opinion at that time, one of the most stupid men ever to wear a naval uniform. He bumbled across and started to give us what he probably believed to be a direct, detailed and concise speech to add efficiency to our forthcoming task. I could see the Boss trying to look captivated and concerned at the same time, while the rest of our small team obtained and applied the information necessary to carry out a search for a ship in distress.

After ten minutes I was able to slip away in order to get the aircraft ranged on the flight deck and checked and prepared for start-up; so I was denied the final pearls of eloquence from our leader. But I needed to ensure that once we had extracted the Boss from the Operations Room, we could take off without delay.

As I was completing the cockpit checks the Boss came trotting around the corner clutching his 'bone dome' and looking harassed, as he usually did after an encounter with the high command. I pressed the start button as he was strapping in and I watched the needles climb around their dials as the gas turbine engine powered up.

The back seat crew checked in on the intercom and Billy added that the winch was serviceable. The Boss stuck his arm out of the window, the Flight Deck Officer acknowledged the 'thumbs-up', and we lifted easily into a hover. I took control and we accelerated away in a steady climb, flying down the bearing we had been given and quickly leaving the speeding ship far behind.

It was about ten minutes past four and although the moon had set, the sky was still fairly light, with the pre-dawn glow creeping over the horizon away to our right. We climbed steadily to a thousand feet and set a speed of a hundred knots while both pilots peered ahead. Within an hour with the sky now lightening rapidly we were able to pick out smudges on the horizon which took on a firmer shape as we closed the distance.

"Thirty miles to run," came over the intercom.

"Roger," said the Boss. I tried to focus on the distant horizon and sure enough, within ten minutes another dark smudge had appeared which quickly formed itself into a small island with a range of hills at the centre.

I eased the aircraft gently down to five hundred feet, all the while keeping the growing shape of the island within vision. As we approached and the upper limb of the sun began to peep above the eastern horizon, I could make out a small wooded island apparently dominated by a low range of vegetation-covered hills running along the centre.

"There it is!" called the Boss over the intercom. "Take us in towards the reef – see – there!" I looked up from the panel and followed the direction of his pointing hand. The island seemed to be surrounded by a continuous reef, about a mile across a turquoise-coloured lagoon. There, smack in the middle of the reef, was a small white-hulled ship. As we flew closer I slowed the aircraft down, dropped the height to about a hundred feet and began to circle the stranded vessel.

She was quite small but sturdy looking, with a bridge and accommodation structure placed amidships and a tallish mast on the foredeck with another on the afterdeck. The foredeck seemed to be a mess of pigs, goats and chickens, all loose and running about in panic. As we completed the first circle around the ship and turned once more into the wind I saw with a shock that the wind was now up to a full gale, blowing against the stern and bringing big waves rolling in across the shallow water to batter the ship on the quarters, driving it further onto the reef. Then I noticed that the ship was rolling and yawing under the incessant battering of wind and waves, causing crates and equipment to slide about the deck and making the derrick arms attached to the base of each of the masts swing back and forth alarmingly.

The Boss spoke to Neville, our Observer. "Call the ship," he said, "and tell them that we have located the vessel, hard on a reef but moving around a lot, and that we propose to attempt to lift people off."

"Already done on HF," came the reply. Then: "Wait…"

We waited, still circling the stricken ship, looking down at the fearful upturned faces. Neville came back on the intercom. "The command says to wait. We are not to attempt recovery until they are on scene."

"Shit!" said the Boss. "I'm going to see if we can get in between the mast and the bridge, then put you down on the deck to assess the situation."

"Okay."

A few words between the two pilots established a method whereby one pilot was going to bring the big helicopter to a hover above the foredeck and slowly descend to establish a winching position while the other pilot would look out for the swinging derricks, masts and ropes, keeping hold of the controls, ready to pull in full power if the rotor blades looked like getting too close to danger.

Very slowly, the aircraft sank down into the maelstrom of whirling bits and pieces while Billy paid out the winch wire steadily, carefully lowering his colleague towards the lurching, bucking deck. "All clear!" he shouted. Power was fed in and the aircraft soared out of the 'hole' it had made and moved away a couple of hundred yards. Both pilots were now soaked with sweat and their lightweight flying suits had changed to a darker colour.

We stood off from the ship for ten minutes or so while Neville disappeared, presumably in the direction of the wheelhouse. The ship continued to rock and swing back and forth but remained gripped in the teeth of the reef. I was beginning to become concerned about our fuel state, when a figure clad distinctively in green flying overalls appeared on the foredeck waving his arms at us. We moved in steadily and carefully over the swinging deck, repeating the same manoeuvre as before. The cool voice of Billy came through the headsets, confidently conning the aircraft into a suitable position to allow Neville to hook himself on. Three minutes later we were heading back to our own ship, still watching the fuel gauges.

As soon as we landed back on board the destroyer, the fuelling hose was plugged in. We kept the rotors turning and I stayed in my seat while the Boss climbed out and walked away towards the bridge.

It was ten minutes or more before he returned, followed by four other men who trotted to the cabin door and climbed in. He looked exasperated as he settled himself back in the cockpit. The fuelling hose was once more connected as we topped up the fuel wasted while we had been waiting for the command to reach a decision. Once the hose was clear I waved away the chocks and lashings and a few minutes later we were once again airborne and heading north. This time it took only ten minutes to reach the stricken ship, still twisting and rolling like an animal in its final agony.

The Boss told the rest of the crew that the four passengers were Damage Control experts and we were to put them into the *Tui Lau* where they were going to assess the damage and try to carry out emergency repairs. They were also supposed to try to receive a tow line from the destroyer when it arrived on scene.

The operation of winching our emergency repair crew into the *Tui Lau* seemed no less hazardous than our earlier exercise; but we were still in one piece as we climbed away and flew the short distance back to the destroyer. We hovered over the flight deck while a light nylon rope was hauled into the cabin and secured to one of the harness bolts. The idea was that the line would be slowly paid out from the destroyer and the helicopter as we air-taxied over the gap between the two ships. It was a complex and difficult task for the back seat crew who had to judge the minimum amount of rope to pay out to match the aircraft's progress. It took quite a long time but eventually the line was lowered into the *Tui Lau*. The Boss reported that the line had been passed and it was then tied to a heavier line in the destroyer which was pulled across the surface of the water to the smaller ship. As soon as it was securely fastened, the destroyer began to wind up its sixty thousand horsepower to try to drag the *Tui Lau* off the reef.

While this was going on I was surprised to see another British warship approaching. The diesel-powered frigate *HMS Chichester* had appeared from somewhere and was now waiting about a mile beyond the big destroyer. With only fourteen thousand horsepower to add to *Fife*'s sixty thousand, she wasn't going to be able to add much other than goodwill to the towing attempt; nevertheless, there she was, waiting to help. I wondered where she had come from.

While we were standing by I thought the attempt to pull the *Tui Lau* off the reef never had much chance of success. If we had succeeded in dragging her out of the clutches of the reef, the sharp coral would have ripped the bottom out of her and she would have sunk as soon as she hit deep water. While we stooged about waiting, I mused that our captain would be unlikely to listen to other opinions, least of all mine.

The towing attempt wasted another hour; and at the end of all the heaving and straining all we had to show for our efforts was a broken tow rope and several damaged fittings in both ships. By this time the wind and sea had begun to rise and the erratic movement of the doomed ship was becoming wilder and more pronounced. At length the attempt was abandoned and we were told peremptorily to go and lift off the passengers and crew.

Thus began a long day of hovering precariously between the top of the foremast and the bridge superstructure of the *Tui Lau*, while one by one, people were winched carefully up into the aircraft. It was a demanding, exacting, sweat-making task for every member of the crew. One of the back seat men would stay down on the heaving, jerking, rolling deck while the other knelt just inside the open cabin door, conning the aircraft over the intercom while guiding the winch wire up and down repeatedly, all the time seeking to avoid the swinging ropes and spars as well as the crates, some still with animals inside, which were sliding about on the deck. The only things we pilots were able to see were the tops of the masts and superstructure, so we were completely reliant on our colleague in the cabin doorway conning the aircraft into a safe position.

The stoicism of the people below, patiently waiting their turn to be secured into the strop on the end of the winch, was remarkable. Many of them had never seen a helicopter before and some had never even seen a picture of one. Nevertheless, one by one they moved forward in an orderly line until they were taken to stand below the roaring wind created by the hovering helicopter, then to be secured into the lifting strop before being plucked off the deck and whirled away through the air until they were hauled bodily into the cabin. At first the children were brought up in the arms of one of our crew but then the older ones, watching what had gone before, began to slip themselves into the strop before being plucked off the deck, grinning nervously as they disappeared skyward.

And so it went on, hour after nerve-wracking hour, loading up with about twelve survivors at a time before lifting clear of the lethal swinging masts and derricks to rush back to the flight deck of the destroyer. There, the survivors were quickly taken away into the ship while another suck of fuel was taken on board before we lifted off again to fly back to the stranded ship for the next load. As the afternoon wore on, the strain on all of the crew began to tell and, in the cockpit, it took a conscious effort to concentrate on keeping clear of the wood, steel and rope which was at every second trying to destroy us, to tear us from the precarious hover over that twisting, rolling, agonised ship and dash us in an orgy of flame and explosion to the deck beneath, destroying everything below and beside us and ending the chances of life for the remaining people.

It is said that ships are live things; and it seemed as if this ship, knowing that she was to die and be swallowed by the sea, was determined to take with her the passengers and crew, and to swat down the roaring whirling beast that was frustrating her in her final intention. Additionally, the wind and sea had been steadily increasing all day and now, huge white-capped rollers were slamming into the ship's side, exploding in a great cloud of spray reaching up to the helicopter and sometimes covering it. We were all uncomfortably aware that while our Rolls Royce gas turbine engine would normally work reliably and tirelessly, it really didn't like being immersed in salt water spray. The salt would accumulate within the engine, gradually reducing its power. It was yet another worry which we really could do without.

Eventually, as the sun was sinking into the western horizon, the last of the passengers had been saved and all that remained was to lift off the crew and the small salvage team we had put on board. As the huge Fijian crewmen left the deck one after another, we could feel the strain caused by their additional weight. It was taking more power and more fuel to maintain position above the ship; and after only six of the giant crewmen had reached the aircraft cabin, it was decided that we should pull away and take them back to our ship before returning for the remaining few. The rate of movement on the stranded ship had been steadily increasing and with it the chance of being struck by some part of the ship or even by a big wave. As we pulled up and clear of the ship I looked down and could see despair in the expressions and attitude of the seven or eight men remaining on the deck. At that point they did not believe we were coming back because they had been able to witness only too clearly the dozens of occasions when the helicopter had seemed to evade the clutches of disaster by mere seconds and inches. Everybody believed that like all gamblers, the more we pushed it, the more likely it was that our luck – and theirs – would run out.

We returned to our deck and dumped the penultimate load of men, refused a short refuel in order to keep the aircraft as light as possible, and lifted off to return to the *Tui Lau*. In the ten minutes or so that we had been away, the men remaining on board *Tui Lau* had busied themselves breaking open the crates which still contained birds and animals, so as we eased back into the hover trying one more time to shrug off our debilitating exhaustion, our final task seemed to be complicated by a menagerie of chickens, ducks, pigs and goats running back and forth around the feet of the men who were to be lifted. In this and the previous lift our difficulties had been increased by clouds of paper, sacks, and rubbish of all sorts whirling around in the downdraft and vortices around the end of the rotor blades. Bits and pieces were shooting through the rotor disc and I was worried about the tail rotor and the engine intake. A single piece of the storm of rubbish now surrounding us could bring us down in an instant if it hit the tail rotor or was ingested by the engine. As I fought to hold a safe hover, my mind wandered. I found myself comparing the symptoms which would indicate one form or another of disaster. If we lost the tail rotor we would spin rapidly out of control but maybe crash over the side onto the reef; whereas if we lost the engine, we would fall without warning onto the ship and the men below.

This last lift from the *Tui Lau* seemed to take a very long time but in reality it was probably no longer than the others. My final view of the ship that day showed that she had shifted even further onto the reef and she was already a derelict. Masts, derricks, wires, rope, crates, deck cargo and loose gear were all flailing around, with terrified animals running hither and thither on the deck. Bits and pieces were falling or being blown over the side. Inside the reef, in the calm waters of the lagoon, three or four small outrigger canoes were waiting, presumably for the storm to abate. Outside the reef, beyond the white surf, the big grey shapes of sharks could now be seen.

I had been strapped into the helicopter cockpit with only a few moments of break since before sunrise; and it was now late afternoon. I was soaked with sweat, exhausted, but with a feeling of relief for the job we had done and the lives we had saved. I had not eaten all day and had only guzzled down bottles of fresh water passed up by the deck crew as we disembarked survivors. Despite my deep bone-weary tiredness I was experiencing a small feeling of elation for what we had done. The Navy had done it, I thought. I was also giving silent thanks for the fact that we had all survived an experience which time and again seemed to be non-survivable.

These were the thoughts which were chasing each other haphazardly through my head as I strolled back down to the flight deck to complete my final task for that eventful day. With Billy our crewman, I needed to supervise the removal of safety equipment, documents and other detritus which had accumulated within the aircraft. Having completed this I was just walking around the outside of the aircraft to see if there were any obvious signs of damage when I was intercepted by a small stout woman of late middle age, clearly one of the passengers we had brought from the *Tui Lau*. She stood squarely in front of me; and as she opened her mouth to speak, I assumed she was going to say thank you for saving her life. To my shock and surprise she started haranguing me, apparently for our failure to recover her luggage. She was American and, I gathered, on some sort of world tour, with a large collection of souvenirs. I listened in awe for only a few moments. Then I turned on my heel and simply walked away.

The next day we docked in the capital, Suva, and the survivors, many of the children clutching small mementoes given to them by our sailors, were led down the gangway into scruffy buses and driven away. The helicopter crew were instructed to get into clean smart white uniforms and were taken to the Governor's house for tea. I can't remember much about the occasion other than that it all seemed very proper and formal. Nevertheless the Governor and the Governor's Lady were fulsome and sincere in their thanks and praise for what we had done.

This experience was in interesting contrast to the second set of thanks we were offered on the part of Fiji. The day after leaving the port of Suva we were to go to another small outer island – Viwa Island – where we would undergo a ceremony resulting in the presentation of a *Tabua*. A *Tabua* is supposedly a whale's tooth and it carries within it great honour and an almost sacred reverence. I was afterwards led to understand that *Tabua* presentations took place in the islands fairly frequently to honour important visitors and to mark great events. However, the norm in each such presentation is for the *Tabua,* once presented, to be handed back with equal ceremony. There are three exceptions to this. The *Tabuas* presented to Captain Cook, to HM The Queen and, now, to the helicopter crew of *HMS Fife* were given to be kept permanently.

The only way to reach the island was by outrigger canoe, or to fly there. We flew. The island was indeed very small and as we approached in the helicopter it was easy to see the sea and the reef all around the island. We were met with due ceremony by the elders of the resident extended family and taken to their hutted village. The men were all huge, with painted faces, amulets, necklaces of shells and grass skirts, while the whole cortege, with us in the middle, was followed by the women and children, all turned out in their colourful best.

The afternoon started with a tea party. Cake – where did they get that from, I wondered? And tea: poured with great ceremony and then served in ancient and precious porcelain cups and saucers. After this we moved to a small clearing where we were entertained with some dances, by the men and then the women, before we were carefully seated for the ceremony itself. Several of the men took in their hands sections of tree roots; and with enormous biceps and forearms bulging, they began to twist them until a juice was squeezed out and collected in a series of half coconut shells. The shells were then taken with more deferential ceremony to each of us in turn. We were invited to drink from them and as I did so, my lips, tongue, mouth and then lower face all turned numb in sequence. We were apparently sipping a naturally derived drug similar to cocaine, a first for me.

The afternoon continued with more small ceremonies, culminating in the presentation of the *Tabua* to the Boss with small but earnest speeches on each side. Since neither side could understand the language of the other it was all set within signs and signals, smiles and gestures of friendship; but it was evident that the warmth and pleasure of our hosts was genuine.

At the end of the afternoon we were escorted by the entire village back to where we had parked our helicopter. As we moved out of the trees we were all stopped in our tracks. The aircraft had almost disappeared under huge piles of fruit, parting gifts from our hosts. All we could give were two heraldic badges mounted on wooden backs, one representing our ship and the other representing our squadron. They were received with as much reverence as if they had been made of gold.

The fruit was a problem. We had to take it all or our hosts would be insulted; and we couldn't explain that we would take it to our ship in several loads. Eventually, with more sign language, we left the two back seat crew to take charge of the fruit left behind while we filled the aircraft with the rest and flew it to the ship, returning quickly for the next load. Finally, after nearly an hour, we deposited the final bundle of fruit on the flight deck and flew back to the island, flying around it, low and slow, and waving to the crowds of happy people running along the beaches or climbing trees before we departed with a big swooping 'wing-over', the helicopter equivalent of a Victory Roll.

Nature, the sea and circumstance had placed over one hundred men, women and children in peril; but the greatest efforts of the sea had been frustrated. One Navy helicopter and four men had enabled all those people to be snatched from the sea and to go on with their lives in the islands.

A Matter of Conscience

The Atlantic crossing had been rough. After the hurricane strength storms of the mid-Atlantic the ship was in a scruffy, rust-streaked state; and a day was set aside to wait in the calm waters off the Eastern Seaboard of the United States while every man aboard, including the Captain and all the officers, worked at cleaning, painting and generally smartening up this representative of the Royal Navy on her first visit to the New World.

Early the next morning, the ship weighed anchor and steamed steadily north up the narrow winding inlet that is Chesapeake Bay. At about nine they passed the United States Training Academy at Annapolis on the west bank; and then, an hour later, the ship had completed the docking manoeuvres to lie alongside the commercial port in the centre of the city of Baltimore.

It seems that whenever a British warship arrives at an American port, the welcome from the locals is enthusiastic and generous to an almost unbelievable degree. Clearly, this visit was to be no exception. The frigate, now with nearly every sign of the recent Atlantic battering removed, was moored alongside a newly constructed city centre complex of restaurants, bars, shops and entertainment venues. The ship was a big attraction with crowds gathering on the dockside from early morning to well into the night.

The crew, many of whom were on their first overseas trip, were in seventh heaven. Men could just stroll ashore straight into the bright lights and music of a sophisticated entertainment centre. As soon as a group of sailors strolled into a bar, they were regaled with offers of hospitality, much of it in liquid form. Girls, already drawn to the excitement and bright lights, were flocking around the sailors. It was a heady cocktail in which the young men found themselves.

Inevitably, since the visit was to last seven days, relationships began to be formed; and by the second evening, individual sailors were being invited to the homes of their new girlfriends. The men had money to spend and so did the girls. The numerous 'Happy Hours', free drinks and generous offers from individuals and the dockside businesses meant that the money, at least at first, was able to go a long way. Of course, this applied much more to the single men who had few commitments at home. After the first and second evenings, quite a few of the married men stayed on board; but some were so overawed by the free, sophisticated and lovely young ladies who were able to offer smart cars and apartments that they continued to head for the gangway at every opportunity. For those with family commitments, keeping up with the excitement, even allowing for the reduced prices and special offers, quickly began to clash with financial commitments at home.

One of these was the 'Doc'. A tall, dark-haired, easy-going petty officer who, running the ship's sickbay, was a friend to every other man in the ship, was one of the first to be sought out to join a group of shore-going sailors. He was visiting the United States for the first time and it would not be an exaggeration to say that he was blown away by the friendliness, glamour and high living that he walked into.

By the third evening of the visit, the Doc was seen to have acquired a regular girlfriend. Reports suggested that she might be a little older than he, and she was clearly much more worldly wise. Some said that she was rebounding from a divorce, but this was probably speculation. She had certainly captivated him; in some messdeck discussions it was said unkindly that 'captured' was more appropriate, as she led him each evening through a whirl of dancing, cocktails, and dinners before whisking him away in her sky-blue convertible.

This continued throughout the visit; and since the Doc was not required to remain on board as part of the duty watch, he was out on the town every evening.

Every sailor and most of their new girlfriends recognise that romances started during foreign visits can have little future; but there are sometimes exceptions to this. When a ship sails, the hour before departure is frequently marked by touching, tearful little scenes on the dockside, followed by women in small groups marking the end of a brief friendship by waving earnestly until the target of the farewell has passed out of sight.

On this occasion, the frigate was to sail back down through Chesapeake Bay for about a hundred and forty miles before entering the massive United States Naval Base at Norfolk, Virginia. The route down the Bay encompasses twists and turns so the overland route is probably only ninety miles – under three hours by car.

It was with some surprise on the evening of the day of arrival at Norfolk that several men with an enhanced sociable reputation established at Baltimore were in receipt of messages telling them that visitors had called for them. These were from some Baltimore girls who had decided to 'follow the fleet.'

At six o'clock, just as Doc was entering the Senior Ratings Dining Room, the ship's main broadcast crackled into life and announced that he was required to come to the gangway. The familiar sky-blue convertible was parked thirty or forty yards clear of the ship with a recognisable figure leaning on the door. It was the lady from Baltimore, who, in all honesty, the Doc had never expected to see again.

The romance, for that is what it appeared to have become, continued with accelerated pace during the several weeks that the ship was to operate from Norfolk. A weekend was spent away from the ship, it was thought in Baltimore, and on every possible evening the sky-blue convertible arrived on the jetty beside the ship.

Several of Doc's closest friends began to become concerned. They knew he was a happily married man with a small child and sufficient demands from his family to use up most of his pay. When it was suggested that he might be getting in over his head or building up unaffordable debts, he quickly shrugged off the concerns of his friends. He said, as did others, that his additional expenditure would be more than covered by the overseas and seagoing allowances to which he was now entitled.

This was of course an illusion. The truth seemed to be that the Doc had managed to trap himself in an affair which he couldn't afford – in any way – and from which he could not see a way out.

After the first few days at Norfolk, mail from home began to arrive; and, like most sailors away from home, Doc was quick to collect his several letters and take them away to a quiet place to read.

He was still disappearing each evening in the impressive convertible but his demeanour during the working day had begun to change. He became distracted, forgot things and quite lost his sense of humour. He became a gloomy, introverted man; but in the busy activity aboard a warship, few people noticed this change and those who did were unable to talk to him. He sought refuge behind an assertion that his affairs were private. This was soon to change, and two days before the ship was to leave the United States Navy Yard at Norfolk, the Doc sought an interview with the Chaplain. He had trapped himself into an unenviable position but he seemed unable to be completely open and frank with the Chaplain despite sensitive encouragement.

When invited to give evidence to the subsequent Board of Enquiry, the Chaplain told the Board that he was constrained in what he might enter into evidence because much of what he had learned had been told with the confidence due to a Priest. Nevertheless, he was prepared to say that the story was not an unusual one for a young man with a besotted admirer in a foreign port. The Chaplain had given such advice as he could, not all of which was welcomed by the young man.

On the last full day in port, all of the ship's company were on board and men were busying themselves taking in stores and preparing for the important series of weapon trials about to be undertaken.

At about ten o'clock, the Master at Arms elbowed his way to the front of the short queue gathered outside the First Lieutenant's cabin, stuck his head round the corner and said, "We can't find the Doc, sir."

"Is he on board?" responded the First Lieutenant, looking up from a batch of signal forms on his desk.

"Yes, sir. The Middle Watch quartermaster confirms that he came aboard shortly after midnight."

"Did he go ashore again? What about this morning? There's been a lot of coming and going."

"I think that's very unlikely, sir. I've questioned all the gangway staff and they are adamant that he must still be on board."

"Have you 'piped' for him?"

The Master at Arms looked rather hurt at the obvious question. "Yes, sir," he said, "and I've searched the ship twice for him. Everywhere except the sickbay and we can't get in there because the door is locked and the keys have already been drawn."

"Who drew the keys?" asked the First Lieutenant, already speculating on the answer.

"The Doc drew them after he came back on board. He sometimes sleeps in the sickbay."

The First Lieutenant decided to let this piece of unhelpful news pass. "Okay," he said. "Make another 'pipe' for him and carry out a search of all compartments including machinery spaces and store rooms. Use men who know the compartments."

In only ten minutes the Master at Arms was back again. "No luck, sir," he said. And then, rather uncertainly, "Do you think we should break into the sickbay?"

"I'll come down," said the First Lieutenant as he headed quickly towards the main accommodation ladder leading to the deck below and towards the sickbay at the after end of the ship. He was followed by the Master at Arms.

When they arrived outside the sickbay there were several men already gathered there. The First Lieutenant reached out automatically for the door handle and rattled it, ineffectually. "Spare keys?" he said.

"Can't find any," responded the Master at Arms, looking worried.

The First Lieutenant stood back from the door. "Break it down," he said.

It took a surprising amount of effort to smash the door lock but eventually the whole structure swung inward. The First Lieutenant stepped through the gap, and stopped in his tracks. He had found the Doc.

The young man looked peaceful. He was lying on his back on one of the two gimballed beds, one foot trailing untidily on the floor. There was a letter on the bed beside him and a crumpled note clutched in one hand. Further down the room the door of a large walk-in locker dangled open, a bunch of keys hanging from the lock. Other cupboards inside this door were also hanging open. These formed part of the 'conversion kit', normally sealed and only to be opened when a doctor was embarked.

The Doc had used his extensive knowledge of pharmacy to raid the sealed lockers, mix together a lethal cocktail of drugs and then inject himself several times with it.

The crumpled, scrawled note addressed the Chaplain by his given name. "Paul," it said, and then further down the page, "I'm sorry."

It would be wrong to divulge in detail the contents of the letter found lying beside the dead man. Suffice it to say that it was a charming and loving letter from a wife to her husband, talking about all the little domestic events that people in love discuss with each other.

The shore authorities had to be informed and very soon representatives of no less than five police forces had boarded the ship, many of them waving guns about and issuing their demands.

The whole ship was shocked. The First Lieutenant gathered some men and ordered the gun-toting police ashore. A British naval doctor was brought from another British ship that happened to be in port, to deal with the body as sensitively as possible with the help of the local coroner's men.

The ship was quiet that evening. Eventually, in some of the messes, men began to reminisce about good times they had enjoyed with the Doc, for such is the way with sailors who suffer bereavement through the loss of one of their close-knit company.

Nothing more was seen or heard of the lady from Baltimore.

Hurricane

We were two days out from Bermuda and heading for the east coast of Florida. Our next port of call was to be Port Canaveral where we were due to arrive one week later. The ship's company had spent the three days alongside the former Naval Dock in the ancient colonial town of Hamilton, soaking up the gentle sunshine and driving away recent memories of the vicious snowstorms which had enveloped the south-west of England for the whole week before departure from Devonport. It had been a filthy winter and every man aboard wanted to put it out of mind.

We sailed out of the harbour at Hamilton with the best Sunday ensign flying and the men lining the ship's side, in ceremonial order. A small crowd of locals together with a few holidaymakers stood on the headland as we sailed past. The frigate looked smart and the men looked crisp in their white tropical uniforms, the only slight element of discord being the line of strikingly white knees emerging from even whiter shorts.

We were due to join up with one of the big amphibious ships which was also crossing the Atlantic and to spend the next week carrying out minor exercises while we each moved steadily across the ocean towards our respective destinations. The big Landing Platform Dock appeared on the far horizon as the hands were being piped to tea at four o'clock, and the first dog watch was closing up. By six o'clock both ships were cruising in close company, silhouetted against a golden setting sun under a red mackerel sky. Half an hour later the two ships were cruising on a south-westerly course, rising and falling to a long swell fine on the port bow.

Our amphibious consort carried two big Wessex troop-carrying helicopters on her flight deck; and soon after dark, one of these was launched to join up with the Lynx helicopter carried by the frigate. They spent nearly two hours with the Wessex carrying out simulated vectored attacks under the control of the Lynx. The two helicopters separated two hours later so each could return to their own mother ship. By the time the helicopters landed, the swell had increased markedly and, with a rising wind, had backed slightly to the south. The senior captain was commanding the amphibious ship and he issued instructions on the tactical net for the two ships to form line ahead, with the frigate leading.

Shortly after this he signalled his intention that the ships should carry out an exercise of 'Officer of the Watch Manoeuvres'. This would entail the ships sailing in close company and changing formation while turning and wheeling together and of course doing all this at different speeds and at night. As the name of the operation implies, these manoeuvres are used to exercise bridge watchkeeping officers and officers under training in real time ship-handling. The orders are passed between the ships by radio, using codes and instructions for each manoeuvre which are listed in a heavy, lead-weighted book – the Allied Signalling Code. A signals yeoman will translate from the big codebook as each signal is received, the appropriate wheel and engine orders are given and it should all be reasonably simple. However, a single mistake causing a ship to turn the wrong way can herald disaster and so everyone on the bridge, from the Captain down, will remain in a high state of alert.

It was only half an hour after the start of the evening's exercise that it was cancelled. The sea state had been rising steadily and the swell had increased in height while simultaneously becoming shorter and steeper. Aboard the big amphibious ship, the rolling and pitching caused by the swell, combined with the frequent changes of course and speed, had been making life very difficult for the crew going about their business inside the ship. In the galley, attempts to cook supper had become hazardous, a fact that had been quickly and forcibly represented by the ship's Supply Officer. The manoeuvring exercise had therefore been postponed to await the arrival of better weather. In the meantime the two ships resumed their previous formation, heading steadily south-west at a reduced speed of fifteen knots, the larger ship following two miles behind the frigate. As the evening wore on the wind continued to rise, the southerly swell continued to increase and steepen, and wave-trains marched over the top of the swell, causing the sea to become confused and lumpy.

It was as the First Watch was taking over that the Captain was called to the bridge. As he appeared at the top of the ladder, a wall of white foam smashed audibly into the front windows, temporarily cutting all visibility outside the bridge. Every one of the circular 'clear screen' units was spinning fast, but it seemed to take a long time for the water and foam to run down the windows from the bridge roof and allow some visibility to the reeling outside world.

The port side bridge screen door was opened by a returning lookout. As the man struggled to drag the heavy steel door shut against the gale, all conversation was drowned by the noise of the wind screaming through the rigging and around the superstructure. Everyone began to realise that we were sailing into some serious weather. The Boatswain's Mate and another man joined the lookout still hanging on to the screen door; and between the three of them, they eventually got it closed and clipped.

Both incoming and outgoing officers of the watch gathered around the Captain, who was now wedged into his tall wooden chair. The two officers stood with legs braced wide apart while they held on, respectively, to the compass pillar and the window shelf.

"Right," said the Captain, "let's get the 'watch on deck' inside, and put the upper deck out of bounds."

"Aye aye, sir," then, calling across to the Quartermaster seated by the automatic helm, "make that so, Quartermaster."

The Quartermaster spoke into the Main Broadcast microphone. "D'ye hear there? All hands clear the upper deck. Watch on deck muster in the Ship's Company Dining Hall. The upper deck is now out of bounds. Petty Officer of the watch on deck, report to the bridge."

The off-going watch had by now departed from the bridge, the clatter of feet from the last man on the ladder just dying away. The Captain sat, silent, slouched in his chair, his upper body moving back and forth as the ship rolled and pitched under the influence of the now angry sea.

"Bridge, Ops Room." The tinny voice emerged from a roof-mounted speaker.

"Bridge," the officer of the watch acknowledged. The Captain looked up.

"Signal from Force Commander, sir. Ships to act independently. They will open out to a position five miles astern and attempt to maintain loose station between five and ten miles astern of us."

The Captain nodded once. The officer of the watch picked up a rubber-covered microphone and said, "Ops, bridge. Roger that." He replaced the microphone and they all stood staring ahead through the spinning 'clear view screens'.

"Reduce speed to 10 knots and alter course as necessary to keep the weather fine on the bow." The Captain spoke without looking round. The officer of the watch gave the necessary orders and silence returned within the bridge. But this was a strange type of silence. Inside the cocoon of the bridge, dimly lit by red and green lights, the men seemed to be looking out on a different world. They could hear the scream of the wind and the crash of the big breaking waves which as they broke were dissolving into a boiling cauldron of white foam with great streamers of spume being blasted from the broken crests by the wind, to fly across the ship and away downwind, disappearing into the blackness of the night.

As the night wore on the weather continued to deteriorate. The noise of the wind seemed to creep into the ship from every corner. Bursts of heavy rain hammered into the bridge roof and windows. The rain came in near horizontal blasts, further reducing visibility; but then it was gone as quickly as it had arrived. Speed was reduced further to seven knots which proved to be just sufficient to allow the frigate to remain in the same spot, maintaining position and steerage way as the now massive waves tried to drive her back. The stabilisers were less effective in the violent seas and the ship creaked and groaned as the bows pointed skyward and the three thousand ton vessel began to climb the wall of the next mountain of water. As the frigate reached the top of each huge wave, she would pause, held by five thousand tons of wild moving water, leaving the long beautiful bow section hanging clear above the reverse side of the wave.

After hanging, seemingly unsupported, the whole ship would tip forward and plunge down the back of the wave, continuing the mad dive until the forecastle was completely buried under water, with solid green water swirling around the bridge structure.

Unbelievably, the frigate would emerge from under the wave, foam and green water streaming in a hundred falls back into its own element, leaving the ship sitting almost stationary in the trough of the moving wave, before starting the whole thing again and beginning the climb up the front of the next monster.

As midnight approached the weather deteriorated further and people had started to come up to the bridge to stand and stare, necks arched back as they tried to take in the enormity of what lay before them. Nobody spoke. Everybody seemed to be enclosed within a curtain of their own thoughts. In some cases, lips were moving. Without conscious thought or realisation men were praying. I remembered something I had heard during another storm years before: 'There are no atheists in a sinking ship.'

But this ship was a modern, powerful, steel-hulled, electronically controlled vessel designed to float, move and fight in the worst of conditions. We would be all right – or so was the unspoken thought of every man who came to the bridge on that dreadful night.

The wind was measured at one hundred knots by the anemometer at the top of the mainmast, over a hundred and fifty feet above the water line. Half an hour later the wind speed reached one hundred and thirty, then a short while later it topped a hundred and fifty knots. That was the last reading. The anemometer had been ripped from its mounting.

During the first few hours of the morning watch, the steady stream of visitors to the bridge continued. Every time we thought the waves could get no worse, they did. Then a really worrying report was received. In highly complex and technological ships such as this one a whole range of computer and other electronic systems are necessary to the routine operation of the vessel. These systems rely on the steady supply of chilled air to keep them cool. Without chilled air, the systems integrating sensors, weapons, propulsion and navigation would overheat, and then they would stop. At about 0200, a report was delivered to the bridge, stating that seawater was coming into the chilled air intake. This was also at the top of the mainmast. Technicians were roused out from non-sleep to fashion makeshift water filtration to try to keep the air flowing and the water out.

Around about this time, short ragged gaps were ripped in the racing overcast and we could see, for a few moments, a nearly full moon. This simply served to show, fleetingly, the full hellish horror of the ravaging, soaring seas, the tunnels of boiling foam, the solid walls of water towering above the ship, and the crazily tilting horizon as the ship was rolled, or rather, thrown and slammed, this way or that.

We were no longer stationary. The satellite navigation system showed that we had been driven backwards by about nine miles, despite maintaining revolutions for a steady seven knots. We could not increase speed without risking real structural damage so we just had to wait until the storm had finished with us.

Dawn seemed to come late next morning. The small breaks in the thick cloud layers had gone and we continued, effectively hove-to, keeping head to wind, watching and waiting. All around us we could see nothing but huge grey and white pinnacles of seawater. Our horizon was reduced to less than a mile, not only by the spray which filled the air but also by the sheer size of the advancing seas. We were a small cluster of wood, steel and flesh in an insatiate cauldron. The only real effect of the arrival of the thin, miserable daylight was to inspire fear – fear of the sheer size and power of the natural force surrounding us and playing with us. We could do nothing more. We were powerless.

The day wore on and conditions outside the ship remained largely unchanged. We learned that our consort, the twelve thousand ton amphibious command ship, had been driven even further backward by the force of the wind against her tall superstructure. In her case she had needed twelve knots driving her ahead in order to keep the ship's bows pointed into the sea.

Inside the frigate some damage had been sustained, mostly by equipment breaking loose, as well as some flooding; but the men had reacted quickly to crises as they occurred and had kept the ship in a remarkably efficient condition. Cooking in the galley was a different problem. Pots and pans couldn't be kept under control even within the constraints built in to the cooking hobs. As for boiling water other than in the smallest quantities, it was dangerous. Despite this, and the never-ending unpredictable lurching, rolling and surging movement, the men trying to prepare food remained remarkably cheerful, producing hot tea, sandwiches and ship's biscuits.

We stayed like this through the whole day, another horrible night and well into the second day. By mid-afternoon, although the sea conditions were still dramatic, threatening and wild, we could see that in comparison with the first frightening night, the storm had begun to ease.

We needed to check on conditions around the outside decks and it was agreed that the First Lieutenant should venture out on to the upper deck, accompanied by the Chief Boatswain's Mate, to check on the state of the ship. They were kitted up in foul-weather clothing, lifejackets and safety harnesses with a tether attaching them together. When they climbed out onto the upper deck and then up one deck behind the bridge, they both said later that it was rather like sitting on a wild, bucking horse. The sea, in every direction, was ragged, confused and dramatic, and the ship was leaping, rolling and plunging as neither man had experienced before.

The external damage was less than the two men had expected to find. Covers had been shredded and guard rails ripped away, while the supporting stanchions were either bent flat or missing. Several other pieces of equipment had been battered and ripped from their stowages and a forty horse-power outboard engine had been torn from its mounting on the transom of one of the rigid inflatable sea boats. Thankfully the engine was still lying on the deck, wedged under the fibreglass hull of the boat.

In the much bigger amphibious ship, now slowly catching up from twenty miles astern, things were not so comfortable. They had suffered the loss of a great deal of deck-mounted equipment while the two commando helicopters, secured, covered and firmly lashed to the deck, had been destroyed. In one case, only the two main undercarriage sections with strong chain lashings still attached remained on the deck. In the vast vehicle hangar under the flight deck, vehicle lashings had broken and two three-ton trucks had waltzed around smashing into other vehicles and equipment before being brought under control. Fortunately, nobody had sustained any serious injury in either ship; and within a further twenty-four hours both ships were again making their way towards their separate destinations in America.

The frigate arrived off Port Canaveral a day before she was due to enter harbour. The ship dropped anchor and lowered a boat to allow the First Lieutenant to inspect the hull of the ship.

What he saw was shocking. The frigate had left Devonport freshly painted in light grey, with varnished woodwork and polished brass fittings. Even in the snowstorm she had looked bright and fresh.

Now she was caked white with salt, the hull soiled with streaks of brown rust and everything looking dull and old. The sea was quite calm with a long and fairly gentle swell but as the boat came alongside the ladder hanging from the flight deck and the First Lieutenant stepped onto the first rung, a six-foot high wave emerged from nowhere, efficiently soaking the officer to his waist.

Sailors are generally not slow to tell tales of their adventures to anyone who will listen but this time, when opportunities arose in the bars and clubs of Port Canaveral, and even later in the favoured 'run-ashore' spots of Fort Lauderdale, they simply didn't talk of their terrible ordeal. They were glad to be alive. They had known the power of the sea and they had known fear. It was a fear which no one who had experienced it could forget.

Mutiny

It started in the after messdeck and not a single ship's officer knew about it.

Gerry Randle, in the view of the rest of his mess-mates, and for that matter in the view of most of the rest of the destroyer's crew, was a shit. He was a big man and the three chevrons adorning his left arm, each marking four years of 'good conduct', gave him an entitlement to throw his weight about, or so he believed. Gerry was a heavy smoker, a boozer, a gambler, and when he could get away with it, an unpleasant and unfaithful womaniser. All of this needed cash; and while duty-free cigarettes were cheap and plentiful on board, Gerry's habits far surpassed his income as a Radio Operator First Class. The title sounded impressive to those who were ignorant of the administrative structure of the Royal Navy, but to everyone aboard *Her Majesty's Ship Olympus*, Gerry was recognised as one who had failed to move ahead from the most basic rating he could hold and still remain in the employment of the Navy. Everyone, or almost everyone, also knew why Gerry had never progressed beyond the bottom rung of his profession. The plain fact was that he was thick, as well as being unreliable and lazy.

Nevertheless, some years previously, a well-meaning but rather naïve Commanding Officer had foolishly raised him to the exalted height of Leading Radio Operator. This elevation had proved to be very temporary indeed. Almost before the leading hand's 'anchor' badge had been sown onto his left arm, the whole thing had gone disastrously to Gerry's head and he had ended his short period as a 'leader' by knocking a young junior seaman to the deck. There had been no obvious provocation and the young man had struck his head on a steel bollard as he fell. Gerry had lost his new rating and been rewarded with a spell in the Detention Quarters, the Navy's prison in Portsmouth. The four weeks in detention had not improved Gerry in any way. His previous captain, now disgusted with Gerry's behaviour, had refused to accept him back in his ship and so the Navy's drafting system had dumped Gerry into *HMS Olympus* without further ado.

Because he was older, bigger and more experienced in the ways and traditions of life in a junior ratings messdeck, Gerry established his presence as a brooding, dominant force within the small community. In particular he started once more to extort money from the 'juniors' – the young men under the age of eighteen who were at sea for the first time. Gerry called it 'borrowing' but he never had any intention of giving anything back.

In addition to his 'borrowing', Gerry appointed himself as the mess 'Rum Boatswain'. This meant that when the 'pipe' or broadcast 'Up Spirits' was made at eleven thirty each morning, Gerry would collect the big aluminium container from his mess and join the queue of other men outside the dining hall to collect the issue of 'grog' for his messmates. He was adept at all the ruses which might gain him an extra share of the mixture of two parts water to one part rum; but the supervising officers were wise to him and he rarely succeeded. This didn't matter that much to him because he was always able to secure an additional tot or so of grog for himself; and if anyone dared to point this out he would declare, loudly and churlishly, that it was a tradition of the Service, or the ship, or the mess. The men got used to it but they didn't like it and most would work hard to keep out of Gerry's way, never challenging him and accepting their unfortunate lot as part of Service life.

Gerry paid no heed to anyone other than himself and from time to time he had been heard to declaim that he was "as happy as a pig wallowing in shit." Such pronouncements tended to take place in the dingy bars of dockside pubs, being preceded and followed by loud, beer-laden belches, while his piggy little eyes would rove around the smoke-filled bar looking for a sailor young enough and small enough to be tapped for money 'to buy the next round'.

Men living in the close confines of a destroyer's messdeck will only put up with so much abuse; and this was the case with the after mess in *HMS Olympus*. Men began to scheme and plot; but everybody was aware that punishment for anyone caught fighting was likely to be severe, and nobody was prepared to take the risk of a ruined career for the sake of standing up to the mess bully. Almost nobody, that is.

Jack Ware, 'Jacky' to his mates, had joined the Navy as an Armourer – a 'Bomb Boatswain'. Later he had changed branches to become an Able Seaman Mine Warfare, and later still he had applied to join the Physical Training Branch and become a Physical Training Instructor. Jacky was a very fit and keen young man with an engaging, outgoing personality; and he sailed through the six month course to become a PTI – a Physical Trainer, or as the sailors would have it a 'Club Swinger', shortened on further acquaintance to 'Clubs'.

There are no 'Able' ratings in the Physical Training Branch. It is considered that what they do is to train by leading, so, on completing the course, each new Club Swinger becomes a Leading Physical Trainer. Jacky was at heart a simple soul who believed that his role was to help his fellows. He was adept at organising all sorts of games, sports, circuit training and competitions, and he was recognised as the ship's expert in every sport. In a very short time after he joined the ship he knew everyone on board and they all knew him. Most of the men also looked up to him and regarded him as a friend, especially the younger men.

Jacky also had a strong sense of justice and, with the special relationship he was able to cultivate with the officers and senior ratings, he was able to set himself as a friend to all. He thought that, on occasion, he might be allowed more latitude under the Rules of the Navy; and to some degree he was right. However, very careful judgement was always needed to see where the 'line' was drawn and to know how far a man could cross it. Jacky's estimates in this respect tended to be flawed and sometimes this led him to assume a closer relationship than was really the case. Despite this, he was a highly regarded asset throughout the ship.

It was a sunny June morning when the incident occurred. Jacky had not failed to be aware of the bullying taking place in the after messdeck and he was disgusted by it. He was also conscious that it was not his mess – not his home, that is – and therefore what went on there was not his business. Gerry had no interest in physical activity and therefore his path rarely crossed with that of the Club Swinger. However, this was about to change.

The previous evening, after a hectic game of deck hockey on the Flight Deck as the destroyer wallowed along unhurriedly in mid-channel, four of the younger residents of the after mess had struck up a conversation with Jacky. Two of the young men had been relieved of almost all of the money they possessed and in one case the lad was devastated because he had no means of making his way home when the ship returned to harbour during the forthcoming long weekend leave period. In the other case the boy felt he had no alternative but to put up with the bullying until either the bully left the ship or he did. He was also sporting a livid bruise on his right cheek, the result of failing to pay his dues when demanded.

Other men joined the group and by the time the hands were 'piped' to supper, a plan had been hatched.

At stand easy, most of the junior ratings had gathered on the Flight Deck in small groups or singly. The after messdeck was empty except for one young man who was sorting through his kit locker, looking for a dog-eared, much-thumbed paperback book. The sound of footsteps coming down the ladder into the mess was followed by a shadow falling across the young sailor kneeling on the deck.

"Lookin' for that bit o' cash yer givin' me?" The hateful sneering voice was all too familiar and the young man recoiled, turning his head and raising a protective arm as if he expected a blow. The blow did not materialise. Instead there was a howl of pain as Gerry deliberately stood on the side of the young man's foot.

The noise coming from the pair on the far side of the messdeck masked the soft tread of a second pair of feet descending the ladder.

Gerry saw the look in the eyes of his victim and began to turn round, but just too late. Jacky was a big man, well able to look after himself and with the skill to stay cool and focussed in a fight.

Before Gerry had turned sufficiently to see who was behind him, Jacky brought the hard edge of each hand down sharply on the side of the fat neck in front of him. This had the effect of temporarily paralysing his opponent. As the fleshy spotted face stared at him, Jacky treated him to a 'Glasgow kiss'. His forehead smashed into the wide nose liberally decorated with blackheads. Blood splashed far on either side causing Jacky to step quickly back, avoiding the red spray. His opponent now became little more than a punch-bag, tottering back and forth as punches rained in from both sides. Jacky was determined to hurt the man but he was equally determined not to break bones or cripple him in any way. As Gerry staggered backward, unable to see through the blood pouring down his face, Jacky continued to hammer punches into the fat torso, aiming them so that they caused his target to stagger back, cannoning into pieces of structure and bouncing back into the next blow. Meanwhile the shocked young junior seaman had scuttled across the deck to the far side of the mess, where he watched the one-sided battle, wide-eyed.

Jacky saw that he had done enough. The blood-spattered body in front of him was only being kept upright by the tier of lockers behind him. He moved forward, close to the broken face, and whispered, "Say sorry to the lad." There was no answer. Nothing happened, so Jacky jabbed three stiff fingers into the soft area under the heaving ribs.

The voice croaked something indecipherable.

"What was that?" asked Jacky, leaning close and repeating his demand.

"S-shorry…" Gerry tailed off. He swayed. He had had more than enough. Disgusted, Jacky wiped his hands on the back of his trousers and pushed the staggering lump towards the ladder. As he did so, a pair of polished black shoes appeared on the uppermost steps and started to descend.

Until now, the messdeck had been empty save for the two men and the young junior. This had not been by accident: it had been planned by the plotters who had asked for Jacky's assistance. But they hadn't considered the possibility of other men, outside the conspiracy, coming to the mess.

The shiny shoes descending the ladder belonged to Leading Regulator Archie Canning. Archie was the assistant to the

Master at Arms and as such was the ship's second policeman. He was a man dedicated to his job and he saw life through the pages of the Naval Discipline Manual. Of course he knew the reputation of Gerry Randle and, like most of his shipmates, he despised him. Nevertheless, he had just stumbled on a scene where a prominent member of the ship's company had been beating another rating senseless. Not only that, but as a 'leading hand', the Leading Physical Trainer had been attacking a man junior to himself in rank. 'Striking a subordinate' was a very much more serious charge than merely fighting.

The shocked faces of the men gathered on the upper deck told their own story as Jacky emerged from the companionway, unnecessarily handcuffed. "Keep clear of the mess," ordered the Leading Regulator, as he led his prisoner away.

A few moments later the 'Doc', the ship's medical attendant, arrived clutching his medical bag and clattered down the steps into the mess. Gerry was sitting on a bunk in a sorry-looking state. As the Doc went to work on him, Gerry was already scheming to get himself out from any official sanction. He could deny any accusation of demanding money from the junior and claim that he had been unaccountably attacked. "There was no provocation..." He formed the words through broken lips as he planned his escape and as the Doc staunched the blood and attempted to clean him up. The young man at the centre of the incident had already slipped away unnoticed up the ladder and along the upper deck.

In the Master at Arms' office, charges were being framed and Jacky was laboriously and carefully writing out his statement. When he looked at what he had written he realised that he had condemned himself. In order to avoid implicating others, as was the way of the 'lower deck', the statement amounted to not much more than an admission that Gerry was a bully and needed to be taught a lesson.

Actually, there were very few men in the ship who did not know what the real circumstances were, but one of the men remaining in ignorance was the Leading Regulator. Despite some persuasion from his boss, the Master at Arms, the younger man was adamant. A crime – a serious crime – had been committed and justice must proceed.

In fact, a similar conversation was at that time taking place in the Captain's cabin between the Captain and the First Lieutenant, who as well as being the second-in-command of the ship was also Jacky's Divisional Officer and therefore responsible for the support and welfare of the man who the Captain was already referring to as "the stupid guilty bastard." He too was not to be moved. The Service would demand retribution and the demand of the Service would be satisfied.

In vain the First Lieutenant pleaded the cause of the Leading Physical Trainer. He pointed out that the assault had taken place on a man who was recognised throughout the ship as a nasty piece of work, a bully, a rotten character, and one who surely had deserved what he had received. But the Captain was not to be moved. He was a fairly young man, new to the ship and yet to come to know the men he commanded, their aggrieved sense of injustice and what they held to be important.

"Sir, Clubs is the most highly regarded man in this ship. The lads worship him." The First Lieutenant felt that his Captain should have been already aware of the high regard felt for the Leading Physical Trainer but forbore to say so. In reality he regarded his new Captain, who was several years the younger of the two men, as a bit of an upstart, a cold fish who had yet to learn how to lead and carry his men with him.

Outwardly however, he had always supported the Captain and had been quick to slap down any perceived criticism from among the younger officers.

"The man committed an assault, a serious assault, and that must be punished." The Captain stared up from his seat by the desk, his lips pursed in a grim straight line.

"Sir, I'm not saying he shouldn't be punished, just that the full circumstances must be considered."

"Must? Must?" shot back the Captain. "Do you presume to tell *me* what I must and must not do, Number One?"

The First Lieutenant looked down, suitably humbled, yet inwardly fuming. "I think that for the good of the ship, sir, and for the Service, this incident should be dealt with sensitively."

"You forget yourself, and your place, I think."

The First Lieutenant thought that any future promotion under this martinet had just been lost. The man was arrogant, self-important and very easy to dislike; but the First Lieutenant made a big effort to put aside his personal dislike. Nevertheless, it showed in his face as he responded: "Very well, sir," before turning on his heel and passing out through the curtained doorway. He strode across the cabin flat and disappeared into his own office-cum-cabin, where the Master at Arms waited, perched on the edge of a folding chair.

The First Lieutenant threw his cap onto the sofa which lined the outboard side of the cabin and flopped down into the chair by his desk. "It's no go, Master," he said. "He won't be moved."

"Well, sir, on the face of it, Clubs is looking at disrating, being thrown out of the branch, and a spell over the wall."

"Yes," was all the First Lieutenant could say.

"I'll send the signal then, sir?"

"Yes, do that."

"Remain under open arrest, sir?"

The First Lieutenant paused for a moment before replying. "We're at sea, Master. He can't go anywhere. Send him back to work but make sure he understands that he needs to keep a low profile."

"Difficult, that, for a Club Swinger."

"Quite. But you know what I mean. What about Randle?"

"He'll live," said the Master at Arms, adding, "more's the pity, many would say. I'll get the Doc to check on him and get the other admin underway."

"Yes, do that," said the First Lieutenant. The Master at Arms stood up, picked up his cap and eased past the First Lieutenant to leave the cabin.

Later that day the First Lieutenant had another uncomfortable interview with his captain.

"He is walking about my ship, large as life!" The Captain was now seated in his tall chair at the front of the bridge and he was shouting towards the front bridge windscreen, his back turned towards his second-in-command.

"He has a job to do, sir. And we are at sea. He can't go anywhere. We need to maintain a routine as normal as possible."

The Captain swivelled round to face the First Lieutenant. "Close arrest, do you hear me? Close arrest until we arrive, and then he is to be landed to the base cells."

The First Lieutenant opened his mouth to respond but as he was once more facing the broad back now hunched forward in his chair, he realised there was no point and if he was going to have an argument with the Skipper it would be better for it not to take place in public. He jammed his cap back on his head, muttered "Sir," saluted the blue-clad back, turned on his heel and left the bridge. The helmsman, who had been witness to the entire exchange, was now concentrating fiercely on the course indicator tape in front of him.

As he started down the ladder, the First Lieutenant caught sight of the battered face of Radio Operator First Class Randle, leering towards him from the flag deck.

At nine o'clock the next morning the frigate nosed inexpertly towards the pier, bumped once against the floating wooden pontoon and embarked on the usual performance with heaving lines, wires and ropes, before resting gently alongside, awaiting the delivery of the wooden gangway. As he completed his inspection of the mooring arrangements, the First Lieutenant noticed a black 'paddy-wagon' waiting on the far side of the pier with two smart Leading Regulators standing patiently beside the vehicle. Their immaculate white belts and gaiters showed that the two men were very much on formal business.

Ten minutes later, the Leading Physical Trainer, now mercifully without handcuffs, was marched down the gangway to the jetty and into the custody of the two Leading Regulators. As he passed, the First Lieutenant murmured quietly, "Keep your chin up, Clubs."

Everything remained normal until morning 'stand-easy' at eleven o'clock.

At eleven fifteen, when the hands were supposed to turn-to again, only one junior rating returned to his post. Radio Operator Gerry Randle could hardly keep himself from smiling, even though it hurt his face to do so.

Petty officers set out from their messes to root out their men but without success. Instead they discovered that the entire after-end of the ship had been sealed off, with hatches and doors rammed shut and no response to shouted demands to come out. One by one the chiefs and petty officers headed off to tell the Master at Arms that the men had refused to turn-to.

The Master at Arms lost no time in telling the First Lieutenant of the situation, first by telephone, then, in more detail, in person. He waited outside the door of the Captain's cabin while the First Lieutenant went inside.

"What?" shouted the startled Captain. Then, more reasonably as the colour drained from his face, "Why?" The First Lieutenant had no answer, so he remained silent. After a few moments the Captain broke the silence. "What are their demands?" he asked.

"There have been no demands, no communication of any kind." The First Lieutenant regarded his superior with barely concealed contempt. "But I expect we can work out what has upset them." Then after a significant pause, "Sir."

By three o'clock that afternoon the situation remained largely unchanged except that a young staff officer had delivered a handwritten instruction from the Admiral commanding the flotilla. The officer handed the document over to the Officer of the Watch, now wearing a revolver strapped to his waist and looking strange as the only individual at the top of the gangway.

The note was terse and brief. The Captain was instructed to call on the Admiral immediately. Within ten minutes the Captain was seen hurrying ashore, looking far from his usual ebullient self and clutching a leather folder. The First Lieutenant hastened to the gangway when he was told the Captain was going ashore, but he failed to get there in time.

Five minutes later, the telephone on the Master at Arms' desk suddenly rang. The voice on the phone refused to identify himself. He said, "We will not return to work unless the

Leading Physical Trainer is returned on board and the charge of striking is withdrawn."

The Master at Arms interrupted. "Why should we do that?" As he spoke he was doodling on a pad, trying to identify the voice, which was slightly distorted by the telephone.

The voice ignored the interruption. "Furthermore," it continued, "there shall be no action taken against anyone who has refused to work, and Randle must be removed from the ship."

"Why?" said the Master at Arms. "You know you can't dictate that sort of thing."

"Everybody knows what Randle was doing and he had it coming. What 'Clubs' did was what everybody wanted to do but couldn't because our rotten unfair skipper would have come down like a ton of bricks." The voice continued while the Master at Arms circled a name he had printed on his pad. "The Skipper and the 'Jimmy' and everybody with eyes knew about Randle but did nothing."

"What will you do if we tell you to get stuffed?"

"We've got mobile phones. We've got legitimate complaints. We'll tell the world."

"I'll get back to you," said the Master at Arms.

"No, Master, we'll get back to you. You've got three hours."

Then a different voice came onto the phone. "After that we will sink the ship." The phone went dead.

The Master at Arms looked across at his assistant. "Stay here." He said, "I'm going to get the Jimmy. "

The 'Jimmy', the First Lieutenant, was hurrying towards the gangway when he was stopped by the Master at Arms who read from the notes he had made of the phone call.

The First Lieutenant listened carefully and then said, "I've been summoned to see the Chief of Staff. Stay here and for God's sake don't allow this to escalate. Also get yourself a side arm. The Gunner has the key to the wardroom pistol locker."

"Aye aye, sir," said the Master at Arms.

****

In the Admiral's office, things were not going well. The Admiral, with immaculately combed silver hair surmounting a hard, weathered and rugged face, was leaning forward over his huge polished mahogany desk, gimlet eyes boring, unblinking, into the face of the uncomfortable commander facing him across the desk. Behind him and to the side, the walls were decorated with large oil paintings depicting long-forgotten battles with battered sailing ships of the eighteenth century navy triumphant. The Admiral's Secretary, a lieutenant commander, sat in an upright chair to one side, while the Flag Lieutenant, a younger man, sat opposite.

"Having a mutiny in your ship is a very unfortunate thing," rumbled the Admiral. "Who is responsible?"

The Captain, showing his inexperience, stepped innocently into the trap. "Well, sir," he began, "my First Lieutenant is weak, the officers are uninspiring and the Master at Arms does not impose proper discipline."

The Admiral's Secretary looked surprised but continued scribbling notes in his shorthand notebook.

The Admiral did not react initially to the excuses being offered, but his eyes hardened and continued to bore into the man opposite. Eventually he spoke.

"So," he said, "a lot of incompetent and poor quality people, eh?"

"Well, yes, sir. Of course I shall want changes to be made and I haven't had a chance to kick them into shape yet."

The Admiral made a steeple of his fingers and peered over them. "So, everybody is at fault but you... No, don't interrupt me." He waved down the Captain's response before continuing, his voice becoming harder, louder and more penetrating as he continued to speak. "In my experience," he continued, "when there is a mutinous incident in any ship, the fault will lead back inexorably to one person – the Captain. In case you are in any doubt, that's you. You come here, throwing about all sorts of wild accusations, showing not a drop of loyalty to any of the officers and men you are privileged to lead." He paused for breath and for effect. "You arrogant little shit!" he said. "You failed to find out anything about your ship's company or your officers, you allow a bullying scoundrel to humiliate and rob the young men you are responsible for – young men, incidentally, whose boots you are not fit to clean – and having allowed your ship's discipline to lapse, you come to me snivelling about the performance of other men."

"But you sent for me," interrupted the Captain.

"Shut up!" roared the Admiral. The Admiral's Secretary was scribbling furiously.

The room was quiet for a few moments before the Admiral continued in a more measured tone. "This is what we will do," he said. "Radio Operator Randle will be removed from your ship and transferred today to work under close supervision in my own Communications Centre."

The Captain began to nod his head until he wilted under the glare from across the desk. The Admiral continued, "Your

First Lieutenant, who is being interviewed by my Chief of Staff, will return to the ship. He will then read the Articles of War over the main broadcast. He will inform the ship's company that Leading Physical Trainer Ware will be charged with Conduct to the Prejudice of Good Order and Naval Discipline but will remain in the ship. He will instruct the ship to clear lower deck and then prepare for sea. All leave will be stopped and the ship will move out to anchor in the bay. On Sunday I will carry out a full admiral's inspection."

The Captain looked as though he was about to speak but the Admiral waved his hand dismissively. The Captain leaned far forward on his chair with an eager expression on his face. He appeared desperate to curry favour.

The Admiral glanced down at some papers lying on the desk in front of him. "A top rate pass out of Operational Sea Training. A First Lieutenant with a gallantry award and a recommendation 'now' for promotion. A 'superior' Master at Arms and an 'exceptional' Leading Physical Trainer. All officers above average. But you didn't know that, did you?"

The Admiral continued. "One final thing. You will not return to your ship; you will be sent on leave initially until the Chief of Staff can identify a suitable new appointment for you."

The Captain actually seemed to diminish in size. He had not expected any such reaction as this and until the interview with the Admiral had started he had been considering the revenge he would exact on the officers and men who had let him down. Now he realised that he had destroyed his career. He wondered how he could tell his wife, his family and his friends that he had been ignominiously sacked only a few weeks into his first command. All he could think of was to splutter, "What about my kit, my things?"

"Your Leading Steward is already packing them," said the Admiral, brusquely. "They will be delivered to the wardroom in the base."

"Yes, sir." The voice of the defeated man was so quiet as to be barely audible. All the bluster and arrogance had gone and the Captain now resembled a punctured balloon, close to tears.

In another, smaller but still quite grand office in a different part of the building, the First Lieutenant was undergoing another grilling; but he was not being put on the rack and as the interview progressed, the atmosphere eased. Before leaving the Base Headquarters he had been informed that he was to take temporary command of the ship and to follow the instructions already outlined by the Admiral. He was further informed that he would leave the ship within a month when a new commanding officer would take over. There would be other changes and this would include a change in the ship's programme. She would be taken out of service and start an early refit, the crew being dispersed to other ships and establishments.

When Jacky Ware returned on board, and the mutiny was over, he was asked what had happened or was going to happen to him. He grinned and said, "I got off as lightly as I could expect." He went on to explain that he had been disrated to become the only 'able rate' physical trainer in the Navy. He had been fined a month's pay and would be denied leave for twenty-eight days. But he would stay with the ship until the refit. He went back to work.

At five o'clock the ship moved easily away from the jetty and backed out, turning to head slowly for the anchorage. The men went back to work.

Gerry Randle was pronounced medically fit and started work in the Base Communications Centre. His reputation preceded him and he became even more of a pariah. He lived in the barracks and spent most of his off-duty time getting drunk in the dockside pubs. His money ran low and he discovered that he could relieve that problem by visiting the trainees' changing rooms at the Sports Centre and helping himself to cash trustingly left in the young men's wallets.

This new enterprise didn't last long, however. Five weeks after taking up his new duties, his broken body was found by the early morning patrol of a dockyard policeman, lying beside the keel of a minesweeper in an otherwise empty graving dock.

The board of enquiry determined that the cause of death was accident, brought about by the man's drunken state while attempting to return through the dockyard.

The King and I

I was a very busy young man. There were two of us midshipmen aboard the Battle Class destroyer and we had learned quite soon after joining that at least one of us was expected to be on watch at all times, whether the ship was at sea or in harbour. I shared one of the after cabins with Dave, the other midshipman and we were close neighbours with another double cabin, as well as the after Petty Officers' Mess. The petty officers frequently took pity on the two 'snotties' and tried hard to make our lives a little more bearable. The leader in this respect was a thin, craggy, genial Irishman. Petty Officer Twomey was a man who felt that the rules were there to be broken and he had been disrated to leading seaman and then reinstated to petty officer more times than anyone could remember. Quite often, as I was staggering back to our cabin, soaking wet from four hours in teeming rain and icy wind, exhausted under the weight of the wet and heavy black oilskin, the door to the Petty Officers' Mess would slide open and the familiar weather-beaten face would peer out, wearing a look of earnest concern.

"Jest step in here, sorr," he would say. "Have a we nip o' dis." Out would come the illicit bottle of neat one hundred and twenty proof rum, carefully and illegally stored from daily rum issues. He would pour a small tot and insist that I drink it down. Then as quickly as he had appeared he was gone. Within seconds my mood of exhausted depression would lift and I would be mentally prepared to face the next task no matter how onerous it might seem.

Since then I have often thought of Petty Officer Twomey. He was an excellent seaman and it was probably this which kept him in the ship. He seemed to me to represent the very core of what the navy had been built on, following many hundreds of his like, down the centuries. He also represented the very opposite end of the scale from some of the stuff-shirt officers in that ship.

Our other neighbours, occupying the cabin alongside ours seemed to go out of their way to make our existence as difficult as possible. Both of these 'enemies' were Special Duties officers promoted from the ranks, both were fairly junior in seniority but not in age and we regarded each of them with hidden contempt. They regarded us with undisguised contempt.

In fact it was a difficult ship at that time in which two aspiring young sea-officers might learn their trade. The Captain, a charming and easy going commander, formerly a successful fighter pilot, had been taken seriously ill during a visit to Northern Ireland and had been carted off to the local hospital, never to be seen again in that ship. The First Lieutenant had taken temporary command and, much to the surprise and horror of the midshipmen, he had been subsequently confirmed as Captain for the rest of the commission. He was an ignorant brute of a man, always ready to criticise or denigrate and very fond of his own importance. The rest of the wardroom was not much better. We were placed under the direction of the Navigating Officer, a fat indolent oaf who came of a well-connected family but didn't have much idea of navigation. For the officers-under- training he was more of a hindrance than a help. His ridiculous and ungrammatical weekly critique of my literary efforts in my Midshipman's Journal still provide me with sources of humour and irritation in equal measure. He did however, inadvertently present us with one afternoon's entertainment when he was chased around the upper deck by his demented Navigator's Yeoman. The poor sailor had finally cracked under the constant nit-picking demands of his flabby boss and had taken revenge. He had raided the Navigator's cabin and thrown everything of value over the ship's side, before arming himself with an impressive looking kitchen knife and setting off in search of his tormentor.

I stepped out through the after screen door onto the upper deck and then retreated quickly back inside to avoid being run down by the overweight figure of the Navigator pounding heavily along the deck. As he flashed past he was sweating, wobbling, gasping and squeaking in fear. Fifteen feet behind him came retribution in the form of a slightly built, red faced and red haired able seaman yelling terrible threats and slashing the air in front of him with a huge knife. It said something for the regard in which the Navigator was held in that he was allowed to complete two more circuits of the upper deck before his nemesis was intercepted and persuaded to hand over the lethal weapon. As the young rating was led away by the Master at Arms, the target of his wrath was left sitting on the deck, propped against the steel bulkhead. His uniform jacket was missing and his torn shirt was soaked with sweat. His chest was heaving, tears of rage were running down his face and he was incapable of speech.

The ship had anchored well clear of the single tiny settlement, in the long sea loch of Seydisfjordur on the east coast of Iceland to take a short break from the turbulence of the surrounding seas. The weather for once was clear and calm, enabling the ship's divers to spend the rest of that afternoon recovering a tape recorder and tapes, a pair of binoculars, a Roberts radio, a record player, two officers' caps and a naval greatcoat. The greatcoat survived its immersion remarkably well and one of the caps was wearable but the electrical equipment, sadly, would never play again.

The Navigator's Yeoman was taken below, charged with various offences and placed under close arrest. His former boss retired to his vandalised cabin and started to compile elaborate lists of his lost and damaged property. Despite encouragement, nobody volunteered to take on the duties of Navigator's Yeoman. I confided in my companion the view that "it couldn't have happened to a nicer bloke."

It was not long after the Navigator's Yeoman's revolt that another officer demonstrated how not to lead his men. The Gunnery Officer, a strong disciplinarian, was charged with bringing the sea boat back on board. The boat, a twenty seven foot whaler was to be hoisted, complete with its crew of five, back up the ship's side to be settled into position under the davits. In ships of that vintage the hoisting required ropes to be run from fore and aft on the boat, along the ship's deck through a series of blocks (pulleys) up to the capstan on the forecastle. The power of the capstan would be used to raise the boat to the davits and then the original lowering ropes, known as 'falls' would be re-secured ready to be lowered once more. When this was done and the weight of the boat was once more supported by the falls, the long hoisting ropes could be removed from the capstan. The order to do this was "Off turns" given by the officer in charge.

The Gunnery Officer, resplendent in his best seagoing uniform, was standing, facing the capstan but with his back towards the position of the boat. He roared "Off turns" in his unmistakable parade ground voice.

"Belay that" said the Chief Petty Officer in charge of the forecastle. He was standing by the capstan facing back towards the boat and could see that the boat's crew had only hooked on one set of 'falls' so he had justifiably countermanded the officer's order.

The sensible way for the officer to respond in a situation like this would be to ask "What's the problem, Chief?"

"How dare you challenge my order!" The Gunnery Officer bristled with fury as he continued to berate the Chief Petty Officer in front of the gathering of sailors around the capstan.

"But sir…"

"Obey my order, damn you! Off turns!"

"Sir, they…" The exasperated Chief got no further.

"Off turns!" The red-faced quivering lieutenant positively screamed this at the unfortunate Chief.

The chief shrugged his shoulders and said quietly "Off turns lads, but stand back.

The two long ropes were allowed to fall away from the capstan drum. One of them flopped onto the steel deck. The other was still supporting the weight of one end of the boat and it whiplashed and snaked back down the deck. The front end of the whaler fell away leaving the boat hanging from the after falls. One man managed to hang on to the vertical stern of the boat while the other four were tipped, arms and legs flailing, together with all the loose equipment in the boat, into the near freezing water.

So far as I could tell, no action was taken against this incompetent officer. In what seemed to be the way of this particular ship, the whole thing was hushed up and never spoken of again, at least not by the officers.

One positive result of the previous afternoon's entertainment provided by the Navigator and his Yeoman was that the role of Midshipman's Training Officer was moved to a rather more reasonable and less pompous officer so life in the

"Gunroom" became markedly more civilised. However the whole wardroom continued to suffer from the silly strictures imposed by the previous First Lieutenant, now the Captain, including the nonsense of dressing up in formal dinner attire, with a stiff 'boiler-fronted' shirt and bow tie, for dinner each night. The grandly dressed officers would hang on grimly to the edge of the table while their food slid around the plate which in turn was constrained by wooden 'fiddles'. The stewards would stagger about with dishes of food slopping around, while the ship bucked and rolled to the heaving sea.

To add to the sense of unreality, the newly confirmed Captain would arrive unannounced in the wardroom to preside over this daily nonsense and regale us all with unwanted tales of his famous ancestors. He seemed to claim descent from almost every historical personality of every nationality – from Nelson to Hans Christian Anderson. The man could bore for England!

It wasn't long after this incident that the ship was withdrawn from the unrewarding and onerous duty of Iceland Patrol and was ordered south. We were to refuel in Campbeltown on the Mull of Kintyre and then proceed at best speed to Portsmouth. Before we arrived in Portsmouth we were told that we were about to become flagship of the Home Fleet, a role previously carried out by the 45,000 ton battleship Vanguard, and unprecedented for a fleet destroyer.

The Captain was cock-a-hoop. He was to serve, cheek by jowl, alongside a senior admiral and he assumed that this was exactly the tonic his career required. The news also did little to reduce the pomposity of several of the other officers.

We arrived in Portsmouth a few days later and our new Captain immediately made a bold attempt to improve morale by restricting leave. Instead, everyone was put to work scrubbing, cleaning and painting. In spite of having been at sea off Iceland for the last month the men took on the new demands stoically. There were surprisingly few grumbles and the ones that were voiced were usually couched in terms of how soon they could get off the ship.

A day later an announcement was made, firstly to the officers assembled in the Wardroom and then to the ship's company by means of the main broadcast. We were told that we would be embarking Admiral Sir Wilfred Woods, the Commander in Chief of the Home Fleet. Sir Wilfred was about to retire and, before he did so he was to be taken on a tour – by us – of the various NATO bases under his command in his capacity as area NATO Commander. We were to visit the Netherlands, Germany, Denmark, Belgium and Norway. The prospect of so many interesting "runs ashore" raised the buzz of conversation around the ship and put smiles back on many faces.

There was, of course, a down side. The Admiral was to be accompanied by his Flag Lieutenant and several off his staff officers. He would bring his own cooks and stewards as well as a small Royal Marines band under the direction of Lieutenant Colonel Sir Vivian Dunn, Director of the Queen's Military Music. The ship was about to become very crowded. The Admiral would occupy the captain's cabin, the senior staff officers would take other cabins, and everyone would shuffle down a bit. For the two midshipmen this meant eviction from the relatively comfortable two berth cabin down aft and relocation to hammocks slung in the passageway leading to the officers 'heads' and bathrooms. It also meant loss of the occasional and always welcome ministrations of Petty Officer Twomey.

It took a week of hard work to clean the rust, salt and grime from the outside of the ship, and then another couple of days to polish everything that could be polished and to paint everything else.

Eventually the Admiral's staff trooped aboard, the Royal Marine band stowed their instruments and squeezed themselves into the after seaman's mess deck, and we made ready to sail, awaiting only the arrival of the Admiral and his Flag Lieutenant. The midshipmen slung their hammocks in the forward passageway. We slipped out to sea with minimal ceremonial but as we passed down Portsmouth Harbour every ship in the harbour saluted us with boatswain's calls, bugles and even saluting guns. The red cross and white squares of a St George's Cross flag streamed out from the head of the main mast, announcing to all and sundry that this powerful looking fleet destroyer was taking a full admiral to sea.

The Admiral seemed a friendly, rather avuncular old boy and we got to know each other quite well as he bumped past my hammock in the early hours of the morning or as he sought me out for a chat and a few guiding tips while I was keeping watch on the bridge. For some reason the Admiral's friendliness towards the midshipmen seemed to irritate our Captain.

The open bridge stretched right across the ship and afforded plenty of space and opportunity for other visitors from the Admiral's staff to come up and take the air. They were a mixed bunch, some of them inexplicably drawing to mind scenes from Gilbert and Sullivan's "HMS Pinafore," The Flag Lieutenant was never very far from the Admiral and I formed the opinion that the fresh faced, and rather foppish, young man was unlikely to be very useful other than at a cocktail party. The Chief of Staff, however, was a completely different character. A small tough looking captain with a deeply lined, weather-beaten face and nicotine stained fingers, he ran the Admiral's programme, and the Admiral himself, with impressive precision and he kept a taught rein on the rest of the staff.

The man who left the most lasting impression was Lieutenant Colonel Sir Vivian Dunn. He would appear, as regular as clockwork, every day at exactly eleven o'clock and again at three o'clock in the afternoon. He was always immaculately turned out in his best Royal Marines uniform complete with medal ribbons, aiguillettes, polished 'Sam Browne' belt, sharply creased trousers and gleaming shoes. Thus attired, he would light a cigarette, place it exactly in the centre of his mouth and pace across the bridge from side to side for half an hour. The cigarette would not leave his lips until it had burned out, when it would be discarded and replaced by another in the same position.

Given that the back of the bridge was on several levels and the penchant of the ship to roll, pitch and heal alarmingly, the Colonel's self-imposed task was not an easy one.

****

We called at Zeebrugge in Belgium, then Amsterdam, Kiel, Stavanger and Oslo before finally heading for Copenhagen where it was rumoured that we were to be visited by a VIP. In Belgium our new Captain told everyone he met at the ship's cocktail party that he came from a long line of Walloons, then changed his mind to explain that he was a latter day Fleming. In Amsterdam he was Dutch, In Norway he had Viking blood and in Germany he explained carefully that his surname was really North German. When someone asked him if he was a Nazi he decided to become British again.

Each port visit lasted for about five days and entailed a good deal of ceremonial. The Admiral would proceed ashore immediately on arrival accompanied by a retinue of Flag Lieutenant, Chief of Staff and a couple of other staff officers. Unusually he was not accompanied by the Captain and it was rumoured that our Captain's offer to do so had been declined. Privately we wondered whether perhaps the Admiral found the boorish man's company as loathsome as we did.

Our final port of call was to be Copenhagen and the day before our arrival we were told that the VIP visitor we were expecting would be none other than King Frederick, the King of Denmark. The ship was fairly smart but this news entailed a further major cleaning and painting operation.

We entered Copenhagen under a bright blue sky and steamed slowly past the ancient Trekroner Fortress towards the little mermaid sitting famously on her rock, before tying up on the Langalinie Pier, in a berth usually reserved for important events and important ships.

The big destroyer was looking as smart as any warship could. With the crew lining the forecastle deck in their best uniforms, the Royal Marine band playing on the small quarterdeck, the Admiral's red cross flying beside the ship's commissioning pennant at the mast head and the best 'Sunday' ensign streaming out astern we must have made quite a sight for the citizens of Copenhagen.

As usual the Admiral stepped ashore as soon as a gangway was in place and, this time, with just his Flag Lieutenant, he was whisked away in a gleaming black Royal Danish Navy staff car.

Two days later and after even more polishing and cleaning, we prepared to receive our distinguished guest. A Royal Marine bugler was placed on the jetty at the foot of the gangway. Beside him stood a young sailor to act as car door opener. Another bugler was placed on the quarterdeck at the top of the gangway together with a 'piping party' of six quartermasters and boatswain's mates.

The rest of the limited space on the quarterdeck was taken up by the Admiral, his Flag Lieutenant, the Chief of Staff, the Admiral's Secretary and Lt Colonel Sir Vivian Dunn. This was in addition to the ship's Captain, the First Lieutenant, the officer of the watch – and, in the background, the duty midshipman – me!

At ten minutes past nine a large black car appeared at the inner end of the pier. It drove slowly along the pier and drew up alongside the gangway. As it approached, the Royal Marine bugler at the foot of the gangway sounded the 'alert' on his bugle and a boatswain's call shrilled the long single note of the 'still' over the ship's main broadcast.

As the car came to a standstill beside the gangway the car door opener stepped forward, saluted with his right hand and opened the door with his left. A tall, distinguished, middle aged man wearing a dark blue double breasted suit and a dark trilby hat, alighted from the car, smiled towards the young sailor and strode up the gangway. As he reached the mid-point of the gangway six boatswain's calls 'piped the side' with the traditional three long notes.

The distinguished visitor raised his hat as he stepped onto the quarterdeck and the Admiral stepped forward, hand outstretched, while the other officers saluted. The important officers were quickly introduced by the Admiral and hands were shaken. Curiously I noticed from the back of the crowd that our distinguished guest didn't seem to be saying much, just smiling and shaking hands.

I was not included in the hand shaking ritual but neither were the other couple of ship's officers present. Suddenly the whole party strode off forward along the 'iron deck' heading for the wardroom and the hospitality laid on there. The piping party and two Royal Marines also disappeared and I was left with just the duty quartermaster and boatswain's mate, contemplating the smart car, which had just begun to move forward away from the gangway.

As I watched, the car drove slowly forward a few yards, before turning to face the side of the ship and park in that position. The driver stepped out, carefully locked the door and started walking back towards the gangway. It was at this point that I realised that the driver seemed to be wearing the uniform of a British admiral. I was confused by this odd occurrence and for a moment or two I entertained the bizarre thought that perhaps kings were chauffeured around by admirals in this country. Fortunately, by the time the driver/admiral had reached the foot of the gangway I had dismissed this ridiculous notion and I instructed the gangway staff to stand by to pipe the side.

As the last note of the piping party died away, the second, unexpected, guest stepped onto the ship, returning my salute with a smart salute of his own. Then he thrust out his hand, beamed at me and said, "good morning, my name is Frederick and I have come to look around your fine ship. Perhaps you would like to show me round?"

I was flabbergasted but I didn't panic as I shook the outstretched hand. "Certainly, Sir – er, Your Majesty" I said. "I would be delighted."

Under the shocked gaze of the quartermaster and his assistant, I strode off along the upper deck, outlining the weapons and systems of the ship to my guest, as though I escorted reigning monarchs every day!

The King was as knowledgeable as he was friendly and by the time I had described the operation of the forward gun turrets and we had reached the bridge. we were chatting like old friends.

I was twenty minutes into my tour and really getting into my stride, having now arrived on the flag deck, when we were rudely interrupted by the Captain and First Lieutenant arriving in an apparent state of panic, from the direction of the starboard bridge ladder. They both looked as though they wanted to destroy me on the spot but they were forced to plaster on false smiles and wait while I finished my explanation of the flag deck arrangements. They had to wait a little longer while the King congratulated me on my "deep knowledge" of my ship and thanked me warmly for the tour I had given him. He shook my hand, I saluted and he disappeared away down the ladder, leaving me to contemplate the fury filled backward glance I received from my Captain as he followed my new friend, the King, down the ladder. I could see that, once again, I was not in his good books.

I discovered later that I need not have worried over any contrived retribution from my awful Commanding Officer. King Frederick had spent the next half an hour and part of his wardroom lunch praising my ability and initiative. Happily the Admiral seemed to agree with him.

I was destined to spend only a few more weeks in that ship. I was posted to a Porpoise Class submarine for three weeks, which was turned by unforeseeable circumstances into five weeks, and then I spent a short period in an aircraft carrier before promotion to the dizzying heights of acting sub lieutenant and a new job as Navigating Officer of a fast patrol boat – the fastest warship in the world.

I never saw my former Captain again but I was rather pleased to learn that he left the destroyer not long after me and was destined to spend what remained of his naval career ashore, in several dull and uninspiring jobs. He was never promoted and I had little sympathy for the bragging bully who felt it was his duty to make my life miserable. I wondered if the visit to Copenhagen had anything to do with that?

Collision

We were part of the usual major NATO autumn exercise which in those days extended from the Eastern Seaboard of the United States right across the Atlantic to the cruel and forbidding seas of the Iceland-Faroes Gap and then further up the western coast of Norway. The exercise was set in three phases. The first phase was called the Planning Phase and involved the ships of the several navies involved congregating in the two or three ports from which the exercise was scheduled to begin.

The second phase was the training phase, where ships and aircraft would go off to the local exercise areas to carry out set-piece exercises and to practice the tasks they were designed for. This would take two weeks, following which the participants would reassemble so that the captains and key personnel could be briefed on the aim of the tactical phase. The ships and aircraft taking part would then be split into two forces. The "Blue Force" would be tasked with escorting a convoy of real or virtual merchant ships across the Atlantic from west to east. The "Orange Force" would be charged with shadowing, then intercepting the Blue Force, to prevent them from reaching their objective.

We were part of the destroyer and frigate screen which was supposed to move ahead of the main Blue Force to locate and hunt down any "enemy" submarines lurking in wait to attack the important supply ships and the aircraft carriers making their way across the Atlantic. In these circumstances it is important for the small escorts to keep their fuel bunkers as full as possible so that if they find themselves in an anti-submarine battle they won't be forced to withdraw due to shortage of fuel.

We left our screening station in the early part of the forenoon watch and set off at best sonar speed to join our underway replenishment tanker which was plodding along in the sanitized water forty miles behind the screen but still well ahead of the carrier force. It would take nearly three hours before we could join the tanker, always assuming we could locate it straight away. As the time moved on the weather, which had not been very good, continued to deteriorate. By midday the wind had increased to the upper reaches of force eight with gusts of up to fifty knots regularly hitting the destroyer, causing the unstabilised ship to plunge, heel and roll with startling suddenness.

The Blue Force Commander had already re-routed his forces to pass between the Faroe Islands and the north coast of Scotland, in order to side-step the submarines which were assessed to be waiting to the north in the Iceland-Faroes Gap. It was also thought that the weather further south would be better. This thought was rapidly proving to be wrong.

We plunged on into the westerly seas which were now becoming violent. The Faroe Islands were one hundred miles to the north and the north-west corner of Scotland was a similar distance to the south. The cloud base was almost on the surface and the open bridge was being continually lashed with vicious bouts of rain driven horizontal by the wind. Conversation was very limited over the roaring of the sea and the scream of the wind as it thrashed its way through the rigging. Visibility was down to about two hundred yards and the radar was being hindered by the "clutter" returns from the churning sea surface. Sea sickness was becoming a problem below decks and several men were already incapacitated by it. The galley could not function properly and the only food on offer was in sandwich form, sometimes supplemented by mugs of soup. Quite a few men wanted only 'hard tack' ship's biscuits and water.

Eventually, at about one o'clock, radio communication was established with the tanker. This led to the discovery that the tanker was some sixty miles to the south of us. We altered course to the south which eased the violent pitching motion but replaced it with an uncomfortable and debilitating roll.

Three hours later, with everybody exhausted from the battering of wind and sea, we sighted the tanker. She was a small Ranger Class tanker capable, under reasonable conditions, of refuelling two ships, one on each side, simultaneously. This day, the conditions were far from reasonable. The two ships steamed downwind in order to provide some shelter for the men on the foredeck who were attempting to rig the jackstay and refuelling gear. A discussion took place between the two captains as to which might be the best course to select for the replenishment.

It was agreed that the tanker should sail down-sea, with the wind and sea on her port quarter. The destroyer would then form up on the starboard side, hopefully in the lee of the tanker, where the sea state should be quieter.

It didn't work. The tanker tried various speeds and angles but the destroyer was unable to maintain a steady course alongside. The tanker turned around, almost into wind, taking the force of the weather on her port bow while the destroyer crept slowly to a position on the starboard beam once more. At first the two ships were able to maintain an acceptable formation, but as the destroyer began to close in, ready to receive the first gun-line, the wind sheered violently round to the north, the tanker slipped a few degrees to starboard and the high bow of the destroyer was driven round to port, aiming towards the tanker. It was only by application of full starboard rudder and a burst of power that the destroyer was able to sheer away from the tanker, and in doing so the sterns of the two ships came within ten yards of colliding.

More discussions took place leading to two more attempts to begin the refuelling. If anything the conditions were worse and it was apparent that further attempts were likely to end in disaster. After another radio conference it was agreed that the two ships should head south at best speed for Loch Eriboll, a long and deep sea-loch on the north-west tip of Scotland. By early evening the tanker was entering the loch followed by the battered and salt-streaked destroyer.

The tanker anchored in fairly deep water and the destroyer slid alongside, with big rattan fenders deployed between the two ships to stop them grinding together. Fuelling started but was stopped after about thirty minutes. The wind had veered further round to the north and was now blowing straight down the loch. A big sea was building up in the loch and causing the two ships to grind and bang together despite the fenders. In fact within a matter of minutes three of the big fenders had been squashed and splintered into small pieces. Both ships were suffering damage along their sides.

As quickly as possible the fuelling was stopped and the two ships moved apart. As the ships waited stationary in the loch. More radio discussions took place between the two captains. Although the destroyer had managed to take on fuel she still had insufficient to reach the nearest shore facility, which meant either Invergordon on the east coast of Scotland or Campbeltown on the Mull of Kintyre. Both were too far away.

It was agreed that we should proceed to sea again and have one more go at carrying out an underway refuelling.

Although still early in the autumn season, the sun was low in the south-western sky, appearing infrequently from behind swiftly moving broken cloud. The tanker set up a course heading north at ten knots, directly into sea. Cautiously the destroyer crept into position fine on the starboard quarter of the tanker. Both ships seemed to be reasonably steady at this point, although the smaller ship was pitching heavily. This made work at the fuelling station on the forecastle difficult and slow.

The men were all wearing inflated lifejackets over oilskin coats and trousers. They also had tethers attaching them to strong points around the base of 'B' gun turret and on the forward bridge screen. This probably saved some of them from being swept overboard as the bows dipped occasionally below a particularly big wave, flooding the forecastle right back to the bridge.

The destroyer started to move forward, edging closer at the same time, until she was abreast the tanker's fuelling derrick, which was by this time trained out over the starboard side of the tanker as far as it could go. The heavy black fuelling hose hung in great loops from the derrick, the bight of each loop remaining tantalisingly just above the bigger waves.

On the destroyer's bridge the Captain, his black oilskin coat shining with rain and spray and his soaking cap jammed firmly down around his ears, had set himself up in a half –crouched position on the port bridge wing.

"I have the con" he said.

A gun-line was fired from the tanker but it flew too high and was taken by the wind to fall uselessly into the sea.

A disembodied voice came from the waterproof speaker. "Cox'n on the wheel sir."

"Thank you 'Swain," replied the captain.

Another gun-line was fired, lower this time but again it didn't make it across the gap between the two ships. It actually hit the side of the destroyer before falling into the sea.

"Steer zero one zero. Revolutions two two zero." The Captain held the microphone close to his mouth with his other hand clasping the edge of the gyro compass repeater.

"Steer zero one zero. Revolutions two two zero." The coxswain's voice was calm and steady as he repeated the order, although it must have been claustrophobic and hard to remain upright in the small wheelhouse below the bridge. Then he said "Ship's head zero one zero. Revolutions two two zero set and acknowledged sir." The confidence in his voice seemed to permeate everyone on the bridge. The ship was in the hands of the most skilled seaman on board.

"Revolutions up or down in twos now 'Swain. No need to acknowledge" The Captain bent down and peered along the compass repeater, noting the precise bearing of the base of the tanker's refuelling derrick.

"Ay sir." The two men had worked together many times as a team and would now almost be reading each other's minds.

The destroyer was in position now. Another gun line was fired, this time from the destroyer, somewhere below the bridge. It flew in a low trajectory across the gap and bounced its way across the tanker's deck, a few feet aft of the fuelling derrick. Men quickly snatched it up and tied on the heavier "messenger" line. Connection had been made.

The destroyer had dropped back by a few feet. "Up two." The Captain spoke quietly into the heavy rubber-clad conning microphone. In the wheelhouse the coxswain increased the engine room telegraph from two one zero revolutions to two one two. The two ships were now much closer and the messenger line had been passed across. The heavier hose line was following and in its wake bringing closer the end of the six inch fuel hose.

"Port ten, steer zero zero eight." The hose coupling was now in place on the fore-deck and the Engineer's team were struggling to connect it to the ship's inlet valve,

"Steer zero zero six." The fuel hose was at last connected and the Deputy Engineer was whirling his arm around his head signalling for pumping to begin. The men around him were hanging on grimly to the nearest structure as the destroyer reared and bucked in the pounding sea.

Fuel began to flow from ship to ship.

"Port wheel, steer zero zero four" The destroyer had been forced slightly to starboard and the Captain was applying a correction. The ship didn't respond.

"Port wheel, steer zero zero two." The compass repeater moved in obedience to the order but the destroyer didn't respond. The angle of the approaching seas and the wind had changed slightly and the bows were still being pushed to starboard, away from the tanker. The derrick supporting the fuel hose was now at full stretch and the hose loops had straightened alarmingly.

"Port five," said the Captain attempting to correct the situation.

Suddenly the destroyer responded to the wheel order at the same time as a slight backing and easing of the wind occurred. The bows angled in sharply towards the tanker.

"Midships," then "Starboard five." This brought the ship back into line with the tanker but the hose was under strain and the gap needed to be closed.

"Port five." The gap between the ships began to lessen and the strain came off the hose and derrick.

For the next forty minutes the destroyer seemed to behave. She responded to the wheel and engine orders and stayed just about in the proper station. The strain showed in the taut lines of the Captain's face as he crouched in his corner, peering alternately at the gyro repeater and at the line of coloured flags now indicating the distance between the ships.

Then things began to go wrong. A particularly heavy wave hit the bow of the destroyer angling it three or four degrees towards the tanker

The Captain corrected immediately "Starboard wheel, steer zero zero six". Stubbornly the destroyer continued to angle in towards the tanker. There were fewer flags visible on the distance line.

"Starboard wheel, steer zero zero eight." The destroyer's bows moved imperceptibly to starboard. At last the two ships ran parallel, if slightly closer.

The captain relaxed momentarily. He took a deep breath and wiped the back of his hand across his eyes. The rain continued unabated. He glanced down at the compass repeater and then back to his left towards the distance line between the two ships. More flags were showing as the ships moved further apart. The destroyer was sheering away from the tanker,

"Midships. Port ten." The destroyer continued to open the distance between the ships.

"Port fifteen" The destroyers bows held steady, and then began, ever so slowly, to creep back to port.

"Ease to ten." The big loops started to form once more in the heavy black hose as the gap closed and the strain came off the supporting derrick. Then the destroyer's bows started to swing faster.

"Midships!" The two ships were moving together rapidly. A loop of the hose was caught by a turbulent wave crashing along between the two hulls.

"Starboard ten." The gap continued to close. "Starboard twenty. Hard a starboard."

"Full starboard wheel on sir" The coxswain's voice cut through the atmosphere on the bridge.

"Oh shit!" said the Captain.

Then the port bow of the destroyer smashed into the side of the tanker. The ships seemed to bounce away from each other and the destroyer began to sheer rapidly to starboard. The heavy fuelling hose was snatched back away from the deck coupling. As the two ships drew rapidly apart the loops disappeared from the hose, bringing it horizontal between the ships. It began to stretch like a huge piece of black elastic and the middle of the hose became thinner then started spurting thick black oil into the sea. At last the emergency release valve responded to a series of hammer blows from a heavy maul and the end of the hose shot over the ship's side, trailing more oil into the sea. The other lines were cast off or cut as the two ships moved further apart. The tanker ploughed steadily on into the eye of the sea while the destroyer continued to turn in a wide arc to starboard, the bows already seeming lower as seawater poured through the ripped and shattered plates of her port bow.

"Stop both engines." The Captain looked worn and deflated as he stood staring ahead into the sea, while the lashing rain and spray streamed from the peak of his battered cap.

"Both engines stopped sir. The ship is not answering her helm" The Coxswain's calm voice penetrated the screaming wind and seemed to galvanise others on the bridge into activity.

The Officer of the Watch picked up the Main Broadcast microphone and spoke urgently into it. "Assume NBCD state one, condition zulu. Damage control parties close up. Flooding for'ard."

****

The forward seaman's mess deck was already waste deep in water. Furniture, clothing and other detritus swirled about in and under the water which was progressively filling the compartment. Daylight shone through a big hole about five feet long on the port side. A petty officer and two men wearing blue overalls and red surcoats were wading about in the water. The petty officer shone his torch onto the hole and down into the water. Waves were slapping against the hole but the depth inside didn't seem to be increasing.

The petty officer shouted above the noise of swirling water and grinding metal. "Right, you two! Out we go. Harris, stand by the door and shut it behind you as soon as we go back through."

Harris moved to the door and, taking a wheel-spanner from his belt, began to hammer the heavy steel clips back from where they were holding the watertight door shut. The last two clips came off. Two men heaved the door open against the water flooding the compartment and then all three tumbled through together with a rush of seawater into the next compartment.

The Engineer Officer was waiting. "How bad is it?" He addressed the soaking petty officer.

"There's a big hole sir. But only about six inches of it is below the waterline. If we can counter-flood aft and turn stern to sea we may be able to do a repair and shore it up."
"Good man. Get the Chief Stoker and the Chippy up here with shoring and a welding kit. I'll get on to the bridge." He moved

75

away, heading towards HQ One – the Damage Control Headquarters.

Two decks higher, Leading Writer Bugg was typing out a letter for the Supply Officer when the collision occurred. A young ordinary seaman stuck his head around the doorway, peering into the cramped office. "Wot the 'ell was that Scribes," he said, using the nickname applied to every 'Writer' rating in the Navy.

"That's the tanker comin' inboard" replied the leading writer, without pausing from his typing.

As the tanker disappeared into the rain and misty low cloud, still trailing oil from the damaged hose, an atmosphere of silent gloom descended on the open bridge of the destroyer. The Captain had moved across to the centre of the bridge and now sat slumped in his tall wooden chair. The clouds of salt spray previously sweeping across the bridge had stopped. The rain fell steadily, soaking everyone and everything as the ship rolled heavily from side to side under the influence of the big seas. Down below, inside the ship, sea-sickness began to take an insidious hold.

Men and equipment had started to fill the forward seaman's mess deck, where water still swilled around, waist deep, despite the combined efforts of two submersible pumps. In the next compartment more men were busily working to shore up the bulkhead between the two compartments. Teams of soaking seamen were dismantling and removing everything they could from the three forward compartments and taking the heaviest items further aft, in an attempt to trim the ship by the stern and lift the bow section higher. The forward fresh water tanks had already been emptied, but to little effect because of the weight of the incoming seawater.

In the radio room the Signals Officer was supervising the transmission of an initial collision report. It was sent with a 'Flash' precedence and in plain language.

****

At last some progress was being made in the flooded compartment. Vertical wooden shores had been hammered into place across the destroyers open wound. Horizontal planks were now being fixed to form a grid, with mattresses and bedding stuffed into the gaps. More wooden shores were rigged across the compartment, braced against the opposite side. This network of shoring was making movement difficult around the compartment but at last the pumps began to gain on the incoming water and the level of flooding started to drop.

The Engineer picked up a sound-powered phone and called the bridge. He suggested to the Captain that if the ship started to move slowly astern it might further ease the pressure on the damaged plates. The conversation was difficult because of the hammering three or four feet away and the sound of vomiting from a young seaman behind the Engineer. He finished the call, replaced the phone and looked into the passageway leading aft. Already, welding gear was being assembled, together with an assortment of steel plates.

Forty five minutes later the emergency shoring and repairs were ready and the vessel started to move tentatively astern and down sea. Mercifully the force of the wind began to ease and the sea followed suit. As the ship gathered way astern, the rolling motion steadied and the men breathed more easily. The galley started operating and mugs of soup with ship's biscuits were distributed.

For the next six days the destroyer steamed slowly astern across the top of Scotland, avoiding the Pentland Firth and passing to the north of the Orkney Islands. The gale began to abate and the violence steadily eased out of the sea. As the ship turned south in the lee of the Orkneys, a second layer of steel plates had been welded across the gash in the port bow and the wooden shoring supporting the bulkhead between the first and second compartments had been reinforced. The destroyer's engines were at last set to move the ship ahead. The Engineer watched the repair from inside the damaged compartment with tension and anxiety showing in his face. At five knots the repairs seemed to be holding well and the ship began the final part of her journey to Rosyth Dockyard.

It took a further six weeks in dry-dock before the ship was ready for sea once more. As well as the hole in the port bow the dockyard discovered that the whole bow section had been twisted to starboard.

Dunsley Wyke

The railway station at Kingston upon Hull was crowded. Two young men emerged from a third class compartment each dragging a bulging brown holdall and a naval kitbag. They looked around for the individual they were to meet, could see no-one and so they set off for the station entrance, struggling under the weight and bulk of their bags.

In the road at the station entrance stood a dark blue, dusty, ford escort estate fitted with an 'RN' number plate identifying it as belonging to the Royal Navy. The driver, dressed in the rather shabby uniform of a lieutenant commander, leaned across to the open passenger-side window and shouted towards the two young men.

"Chuck your kit in the boot and hop in the back, lads," he called. The rear door of the estate was opened and the four bags dumped inside. Their owners slid into the back seats, as directed. Before the final door had been shut, the car was in gear and moving.

"Welcome to Hully Gully," called the driver over his shoulder. "So you two are joining *Jutland?* " The car sped across an intersection on the last of the amber traffic light.

"What do you call yourselves?"

"Harry, sir."

"Tom, sir"

"OK, The programme is this. We go back to my base; get a cup of tea, sort out your kit for seagoing, then we go to Harry Ramsden's for the best feed of fish and chips you'll ever have, and after that I'll take you down to the docks and settle you in to the *Dunsley Wyke.*

"*Dunsley Wyke*, sir? What's that?" Harry asked the question.

"She's an antique trawler and she's your transport out to the fishing grounds."

The two passengers sat waiting for more.

After a few more moments of slightly erratic driving, the car stopped, accompanied by a squeal of brakes and a cloud of dust. The two passengers climbed out, recovered their bags from the back of the car and followed the driver into a nondescript single story building.

Ten minutes later they were all seated in comfortable, well-worn armchairs, sipping tea from heavyweight china mugs.

"So," said the lieutenant commander, "You're both brand new midshipmen, off to sea and to put the world to rights, eh?"

Harry nodded. Tom said "yes sir."

"Lose the 'sir ' bit while you're here lads. It makes me feel old." The lieutenant commander shrugged out of his jacket and threw it onto a fourth armchair in the far corner of the room.

"What exactly do you do here?" asked Harry.

"Fishery Liaison Officer. 'Fish basher' to the locals. I keep up to speed with the deep sea skippers. Find out what they've seen up north and sometimes I take my cameras and go for a little trip. Then I keep my bosses at Naval Intelligence happy with current rumours or whatever. It keeps me from getting bored. More tea?"

On the advice of Lieutenant Commander Gerry Blunt the midshipmen went into the next room which seemed to be an unused bedroom, tipped out the contents of their baggage and began to rearrange their kit so that what they were likely to need during their journey in the trawler was put into the holdalls and the rest was returned to the kitbags. They were then given a tour of what Gerry Blunt described as his workshop, which was a back room fitted out as a photographic dark room, complete with taps, washbasins, trays and jars of photographic chemicals. The whole room was criss-crossed by lines of string with rolls of negatives hanging up to dry. A plastic topped table was covered with black and white photographs of warships, submarines and occasionally fishing trawlers festooned with arrays of aerials.

"He's a spy" said Harry quietly, when they were alone a little later.

"Yes, but he's our spy," retorted Tom.

****

The visit to Harry Ramsden's Fish and Chips proved as satisfying as they had been told and, although mid-summer, it was fairly dark as the two midshipmen were driven down to the fish quays. They drove past several quite impressive looking ocean-going trawlers and stopped eventually beside a wooden walkway leading down to what seemed at first to be an empty quay. As they approached, the shape of a smaller and distinctly ancient looking vessel formed itself out of the darkness.

The tide was low so the only parts of the trawler at first visible above the stone quay were two masts with derricks attached, the top half of the wheelhouse structure and a single tall funnel. As they came nearer the excitement previously dominating the thoughts of the midshipmen tailed away and disappeared. They were looking at a very old and dilapidated vessel which would have seemed more at home in a museum. Most of the structure above the deck seemed to be made of wood. The wheelhouse looked like a square, two-storey, chicken shed surrounded at the upper level with windows, several of which seemed to be cracked. Everything seemed old with red rust dominating most of the fittings and with piles of ropes and netting cluttering the deck space. The whole ship seemed to sit under a cloud redolent of decayed fish.

Whistling happily, Gerry Blunt led the way down a narrow, swaying, gangplank and hopped onboard, stepping nimbly across a heap of netting which exuded the stink of long-dead fish. Noses wrinkled against the smell, the two midshipmen followed in silence.

Gerry stopped by a door set in the back of a structure which supported the wheelhouse. "This way lads. I'll go down and you can pass me your kit." He clattered quickly down the stairs with his back to the steps, turned and stretched his arms out to receive the bags.

A couple of minutes later the two midshipmen were being introduced to their individual homes for the next few weeks. The crew's mess they were standing in stretched across the ship from side to side. The outer and rear bulkheads were lined with ample curtained bunks set in tiers of three. Sets of steel lockers filled the space below the lowest bunks. The centre of the room was occupied by a large battered wooden table, decorated with dozens of sets of initials carved into its surface. The table was surrounded with a dozen mismatched chairs, almost all of them damaged. The room lacked ventilation and was infused with a clinging odour of ancient sweat. There were eighteen bunks in all and Gerry walked towards a tier of three on the after bulkhead. "None of these are in use," he said, "You get to take your pick.

"How big is the crew?" asked Tom.

"Skipper, Mate, who have cabins under the wheelhouse, and ten men. That includes the cook and the engineer. So there are eight fishermen. They usually work in two watches. They'l soon find something for you two to do."

Each bunk was equipped with a worn sleeping bag which did seem fairly clean. Within ten minutes of the departure of their guide, each midshipman was tucked into a sleeping bag behind the drawn bunk curtain, sleeping soundly. Neither of them had thought to ask where the rest of the crew were.

As the night wore on into the early hours of the morning, men came stumbling down the gangplank, clattering down the ladder and, some noisily, some less so, climbed into their bunks and fell asleep. The mess deck vibrated to a cat's chorus of inebriated snores.

It was movement that awoke Tom. This and the solid thump of a diesel engine told him that the ship was underway. He crawled out of his sleeping bag and manoeuvred himself down to the deck. Almost all of the other bunks were curtained and the noise of snoring suggested that they were still occupied. He realised that he had no idea of the location of either the heads or bathrooms. In fact there were no bathrooms –just an erratic shower.

Harry dropped down from the top bunk, rubbed his eyes and stood blinking beside Tom. "Where's the heads?" he asked.

As Tom tried to remember what Lieutenant Commander Gerry Blunt had told them about the layout and essential facilities he saw a pair of scuffed boots descending the ladder from the main deck. The boots were followed by a wiry body surmounted by a weather-beaten face, tanned and wrinkled to seem much older than the man really was. "Over there, through the door on the port side," he said, jerking his head towards the direction he was describing. Harry set off for the doorway while Tom stared at the man.

"I'm Geordie. I'm the mate, and I'll teach you the fishin' trade if you've a mind." He walked back towards the ladder and called over his shoulder, "get yerselves sorted an' then come up to the wheelhouse. Fifteen minutes, OK?" Tom nodded.

Twenty minutes later, clad now in 'Number Eight' naval working dress shirt and trousers, the midshipmen arrived on the bridge. Geordie looked pointedly at his wristwatch but then turned towards another man who was standing beside the ship's wheel. They were on the open sea with no sign of land. Apart from the two men on the bridge there was no sign of any other people.

"Skipper, these are our two passengers," said Geordie by way of introduction.

The Skipper turned towards them. "I hope you mean new working hands," he said. He stood for a moment quietly appraising the newcomers. He was at least ten years older than the mate and whereas Geordie was wiry, the Skipper was more thickset, a muscular man now tending to run to fat in places. He had the same lined, weather beaten face as the Mate but a more powerful appearance with two small coal-black eyes above a luxuriant black beard.

He stuck out a hand. "Welcome aboard."

They each shook hands rather formally then Tom ventured a question. "Where is everybody?" he said. "I mean where are the crew?"

Crinkled lines appeared briefly below the black eyes, as the skipper grinned beneath his beard. "Maybe that's you. You are the crew."

The midshipmen just stood there, looking shocked.

Geordie broke the silence. "Nah," he said, "Skipper's havin' you on. His joke, see. Most of the lads are sleeping it off. They'd been on the piss, big time last night. Hardly find their way back aboard, some of them. It's only me, the Skipper, Cookie an' Engines as is awake. The rest'll be around when they gets hungry. Wanna see the ship? Follow me".

For the next forty minutes the midshipmen trailed around behind the Mate while he explained the location of the galley, the main and forward heads, the showers that worked and those that didn't, the fish hold, how the trawl gear was rigged, who did what and the few tasks they would be able to help with, most of which seemed to consist of ice breaking and packing gutted fish in the cold room.

Before he left them, Geordie took them down to the galley, indicated 'Cookie' , who nodded silent acknowledgement and then delved in a wooden locker, emerging with two enamelled metal dishes. He passed one to each man. "These," he said, "are your plates. You look after them, keep them clean and bring them to each meal. Don't lose them. If you lose them you don't eat, because there are no more. Incidentally you wipe them clean. Don't use fresh water – it's precious. And don't try washing them over the side. That way you'll lose them. Got it?"

They took the plates and each signified that they had 'got it'.

****

As the Trawler steamed steadily north the weather started to deteriorate. Five days later they were approaching the fishing grounds to the south of Iceland and they started running a trawl as they continued to the north-west at a slower speed. The weather by this time seemed to have settled into a pattern of westerly gales, each separated from the next by an interval of only a few hours. During these breaks in the wind the seas continued to run high and the two young men had to deal with bouts of sea-sickness in addition to the other hardships of the noisy, lurching and heaving life aboard. After a while they both became more used to the constant movement and the sickness retreated. They started eating properly and were introduced to the practical difficulty of having only one plate to accommodate three courses.

At first they recoiled from the process of having a ladle full of soup surmounted by a main course of fish and potatoes with the whole thing topped off with prunes and custard, or something similar. The fish and potatoes were both fresh, in the case of the fish, often caught that day, but all of the rest came in tins.

The trawler continued the routine of trundling round the fishing grounds, with weather varying from bad to very bad and the newcomers settled in to a routine of working in the fish hold, watching from the deck to see the trawl opened, doing a bit of Decca navigation and chart work on the bridge and even beginning to enjoy their strange eating arrangements.

They found that the constant movement of the small lively trawler resulted in them being permanently tired so that they were each almost asleep by the end of their working days. Sometimes, when the trawls were light, these days went on deep into the night. This routine continued for the next five weeks by which time the *Dunsley Wyke* had followed the trawler fleet around to the north of Iceland

Suddenly, as though the two midshipmen had only just been remembered, a radio call was received from the Duty Destroyer. *HMS Jutland*, their destination, was heading towards the *Dunsley Wyke* and the two midshipmen were to be ready to be transferred to the destroyer early the following morning.

The last trawl of the day was hauled in at 1800 that evening. The crew went to supper and as soon as they had finished in the fish hold the midshipmen started to sort out the uniforms they would need for the following morning.

Harry stood looking in horror at his best uniform which had lain folded (he thought) and forgotten in the bottom of his kitbag. He rooted further through the contents of the kitbag and pulled out his second best 'seagoing' uniform. It was crumpled and creased, "like a dishrag," said Tom before he found his own uniforms in a similar state. Harry found some wire coat hangers and set the reefer jackets on them which made them look even more horrible with the added problem of traces of green mould adorning parts of the cloth.

By nine o'clock that evening both young men were despairing. Every attempt to improve the uniforms by sponging, stretching and wearing them had failed. The only success in improving the appearance of the fine doeskin cloth was in removing the green mould.

Tom started to ask around to see if anyone had an iron or an ironing board. The responses consisted mostly of wry grins and shaking heads.

About an hour later the Engineer emerged from the engine room and sat pensively watching the efforts of the midshipmen while smoking his pipe. After a while he walked over to Harry, nudged him with an elbow and said, I may be able to help you there, but I'll need a word with the Skipper first. He disappeared up the ladder in the direction of the wheelhouse while the vain efforts continued with the stubborn uniform suits. Ten minutes later he was back, pipe still clamped firmly between his teeth but now issuing renewed clouds of grey smoke from a fresh plug of tobacco.

An hour later, the engine was stopped and the trawler came to rest, rolling steadily back and forth. The Engineer disappeared back down into his engine room where he switched off the oil burners heating the boiler and, after waiting for a while for the machinery to cool, he began to disconnect one of the huge nuts and bolts connecting the crankshaft to the steam cylinders. Shortly after this he reappeared in the mess deck clutching the big bolt, the top of which was flat and measured about six inches across.

Followed by both Tom and Harry he took the bolt to the galley where it was placed on top of the stove. It heated up quite quickly and was then carefully removed from the top of the stove, wrapped in a piece of cloth and handed to the midshipmen. The uniform suits were spread out on the mess deck table and the pressing process was begun.

It took another hour and a half involving repeated trips back to the galley stove before the task was complete. Two uniforms seemed quite presentable and the other two, the seagoing uniforms were passable. After this the engineer set off in a cloud of warm gratitude from the owners of the newly pressed suits.

The slight euphoria was, however, balanced to some degree by the grumbles emerging from behind curtained bunks as the rolling of the stationary ship increased with the rising sea. Another hour passed and by midnight the engine con-rod had been reassembled, the boiler fired up and the trawler was once more moving forward with an easy motion, through the sea.

****

Early next morning the big destroyer came creaming up over the horizon at an impressive speed. Within half an hour it had stopped about a hundred yards upwind of the trawler, now stationary once more and rolling on the restless swell. An open top, inflatable rubber dinghy was lowered over the side attached to a long rope. The rope was paid out by some men on the destroyer's quarterdeck and allowed to drift quickly down towards the trawler. At first it appeared to be about to pass ahead of the trawler but the skipper moved his ship slowly forward to intercept the dinghy which was now bouncing and twisting alarmingly in the wind.

Eventually the dinghy was brought alongside the trawler and held there while the two white-faced midshipmen were helped to climb down into the frail looking rubber boat. As soon as their gear had been handed down, the rope started to tighten as the men on the destroyer began to haul the small rubber boat back across the turbulent gap between the two ships.

The occupants of the dinghy had wedged themselves in as best they could, each with one hand hanging on grimly to the side of the dinghy and the other white knuckled hand grasping their worldly goods, which seemed to be under threat of being washed away with each lurch of the small boat.

The journey between the two ships was slow and horrible. Breaking seas washed over the dinghy, repeatedly soaking the occupants and destroying their efforts of the previous night with their uniforms. After what seemed a very long time, the dinghy was drawn into the lee of the destroyer and manoeuvred alongside a rope ladder dangling from the quarterdeck. Hands reached down and took the soaking, salt encrusted luggage as it was passed up. The two midshipmen, also soaking wet, climbed, one after the other onto the destroyer's quarterdeck. They each had the presence of mind to clamp their dripping uniform caps on their heads and, with trembling frozen hands, to attempt a formal salute as they entered their new ship for the first time.

Standing in front of them was the destroyer's First Lieutenant, a thick set, coarse featured man wearing an immaculately pressed uniform. He had a brass bound telescope tucked under his left arm and everything about him seemed to gleam. He scowled at the two new arrivals, who were standing in pools of water dripping from their clothes, ignored their salutes and said "How dare you come aboard my ship looking like that." The new midshipmen were later to discover that he was an ignorant brute of a man who had already reached the pinnacle of his career and was in no way representative of the officer corps of the Navy.

A few hundred yards away, a long toot on the whistle and a puff of black smoke signalled the departure of the *Dunsley Wyke*.

The Chase

We had just completed a major refit and were about to re-enter the fleet as one of the most up-to-date and effective frigates in the Royal Navy. The huge sum of money spent on the ship over the previous year had produced two of the most effective missile systems in the world, as well as an anti-submarine torpedo system that could be truly regarded as an underwater guided missile. We carried a modern Lynx helicopter capable as both an anti-submarine and anti-surface weapons system in its own right. We were potentially one of the most effective modern warships afloat.

First, however, before we could enter the fleet as a fully operational unit we would have to prove ourselves and this meant that each of the sensors and weapon systems would have to be tested , calibrated and then tested again under all possible and predictable circumstances. We and the embarked boffins would have to prove that every sensor and weapon that had been installed at such great expense would meet and even surpass its design parameters. It would be a long process because everything would need to be tested independently and then as part of its operational system. Real targets, aircraft, ships and submarines , would need to be deployed so that we could be convinced that our systems would do what they were supposed to do.

It was a crisp November morning as the last ropes were slipped from the jetty in the South Yard of Devonport Naval Base. The ship and her company were untried after nearly two years in dockyard hands, so everything was being done methodically and with great care. Nobody wanted a foul-up at this important juncture. Only the previous day a row had arisen with the dockyard riggers over the removal of scaffolding which surrounded the radar aerials above the bridge. The 'dockyard mateys' had prevaricated about dismantling the scaffolding poles for weeks past and now they were going down the usual route of finding reasons for not doing the work until it was forced into overtime. This was very frustrating but nobody was really surprised. The dockyard riggers were a militant lot and after removing every argument for not doing the work they had finally dug in their heels and demanded that the small gangway provided by the ship should be replaced by a huge dockyard construction, which would need to be placed in position by a heavyweight crane, and which was probably sufficiently robust to withstand a near-miss by a thousand pound bomb.

Eventually, patience snapped. The ship's First Lieutenant called the Charge-Hand over and told him bluntly that if the dismantling had not started within the next half hour, the ship's crew would do it themselves.

There was an instantaneous and unhelpful reaction. All of the rigging gang downed tools and plodded off in the direction of the dockyard canteen. Twenty minutes later they were back, voicing outrage at the fact that smiling sailors were already carrying scaffold poles ashore and dumping them in an untidy heap on the jetty.

Harsh words were exchanged as the scaffolding tower above the bridge grew smaller and the pile of poles on the jetty grew bigger. Realising that they were not going to win and that they were losing money, the riggers spontaneously marched onboard, rigged up a very hazardous looking plank between ship and shore and, with demonstrable bad grace they quickly completed the job the sailors had started.

We were, at last, ready to sail!

****

We eased away from the jetty, going astern until the gap between the ship and her recent home had widened sufficiently to allow a slow and stately turn to port, with the starboard engine at half ahead and the port engine at slow astern. A motley collection of dockyard workers, officers and men from other ships and others from the dockyard hierarchy and the staff of Flag Officer Plymouth had gathered to see us off.

At last, with a toot on the ship's siren, we were on our way. We picked up speed as we passed through the narrows, piping a salute to ships and admirals as we passed them. Half an hour later we were through the Eastern Entrance and turning to head south-west as the lighthouse and concrete breakwater dropped away behind us. We settled onto a south-westerly course at the economic speed of fifteen knots. The trials team assembled in the wardroom with the key ship's officers to explain how the ship's 'state of the art' passive sonar was to be analysed and assessed to see what it could really do in the open ocean.

The big sonar set itself, where it was fitted and the information it was expected to provide was still highly classified so the briefings all took place behind closed doors.

It took 24 hours to reach the area of the south-western approaches where the water was deep enough for the trial to take place. A few hours before this we were to make contact with a Trafalgar class nuclear attack submarine, which would act as a target for our sonar. This type of submarine had been chosen for the role of target because it was very quiet when underwater and consequently difficult to detect.

About twelve hours after leaving Devonport, when everything had settled down nicely and the First Lieutenant was just completing "evening rounds" an unusual report was received on the bridge.

"Bridge, Ops Room."

The Officer of the Watch cast around for the correct microphone with which to reply. He was still getting used to the layout of the bridge fittings. Eventually he said, "bridge. Go ahead,"

"Bridge, ops. Sonar contact bearing two two zero, twelve miles."

The Officer of the Watch thought for a moment and then said, "Bridge, roger. Keep me informed please."

"Roger."

The Officer of the Watch picked up the intercom microphone to the Captain's cabin. "Captain, sir. Officer of the Watch speaking. Ops is reporting a sonar contact about twelve miles ahead. I think it may be our nuclear playmate." He waited for the reply.

"I'll come up." One minute later the Captain appeared at the top of the bridge ladder. He was an experienced seaman but he was acutely aware that he had not served at sea for nearly five years and he didn't want any problems on day one. The first possible problem in his mind was that the rendezvous with the friendly nuclear submarine was not due to take place until the following afternoon. That position was still three hundred miles further on. He nodded to the Officer of the Watch and climbed into his chair.

"Bridge, ops." The speaker sprang into life again. "Sonar contact assessed as possible submarine."

The Captain raised his eyebrows as he picked up the microphone. "Can you ask the Ops Officer to come to the Operations Room please."

"Ops here sir." The answer was immediate.

"Have you had a look at this contact?"

"yes sir. Range is now seven miles, sitting right in our path. We have good passive contact but we are not transmitting on active sonar. The contact is moving very slowly to the south, no cavitation but we are picking up what I think is a bit of machinery noise. I think we will be able to classify it 'probable submarine' in a few moments."

"Good. Let me know as soon as you have re-classified." The Captain replaced the microphone in its clip.

Ten minutes passed, then another five. On the bridge, nobody spoke.

"Contact now classified probable submarine. Assessed as Soviet Foxtrot Class." The suddenness with which the familiar voice of the Operations Officer boomed out of the overhead speaker startled everyone.

"I'm coming down." The Captain eased himself out of his chair and moved towards the bridge ladder.

****

As he entered the operations room the Captain sensed through the red-lit gloom that the place was busy. He made his way carefully across to the command console and slid onto a seat, peering down at the huge electronic display. He waited for his eyes to complete their adjustment from the evening brightness of the bridge while identifying the relative positions of the electronic symbols in front of him. A white-shirted arm appeared beside him, fingers pointing to the horizontal screen.

"There he is, sir – and that's his original position . Hasn't moved very far and I don't think he was just lying there by accident. He's trying to keep quiet but I think he is waiting for us to pass by so he can pick up our trail and see what we're up to."

"Any news of our own clockwork mouse, John?"

"*Tiptoe* is supposed to rendezvous with us at oh-eight – double-oh tomorrow morning. That's eighty miles from our present position. She's supposed to be on the surface but that is going to make her temporarily blind and vulnerable. I think we should get off a 'Flash' signal, changing the rendezvous and telling her to remain submerged."

The Captain stayed still for a moment, eyes wandering around the electronic plotting table. "Yes, do that," he said, then, as an afterthought, "is there anything else around?"

"Not much, nothing really interesting that is; although we did pass a bulk carrier belonging to 'Ivan' a while back. He was going fairly slowly.

The Captain reached for the bridge intercom microphone. "Officer of the Watch, Captain. I want you to come fifty degrees to starboard and increase speed to twenty-two knots. Check that there is nothing in the way and tell the Engineer what is intended. Give him whatever notice he needs before coming up in speed."

"Aye aye sir."

Turning back to the Operations Officer, the Captain said, "Mark the plot and hang on to the contact as long as you can. I'm going to move away fast for a couple of hours and see what happens. I have a nasty feeling that this fellow is not there by accident and I think he wants to be an extra observer at our trial. We need to avoid that."

The Operations Officer nodded agreement.

"The big worry," continued the Captain, "is how the hell does he know that we are going to do something interesting and where we are going to do it."

Three hours later the frigate had moved nearly seventy miles away from the position of the submarine contact and forty miles to the north of their original projected track. An acknowledgement of the change in plans had been received, via Fleet Headquarters at Northwood, from the nuclear attack submarine *HMS Tiptoe* and everyone was ready to begin the capability assessment of the new sonar system. The contact assessed as a Soviet Foxtrot class conventional submarine had been lost an hour after the frigate had begun to clear the area at high speed but a datum had been established which was being regularly updated at the submarine's estimated underwater speed.

****

HMS Tiptoe registered her presence by firing a green flare from underwater, the Lynx helicopter returned to the frigate having established the identity of all the surface contacts in this remote part of the Western Approaches, and the trial began.

Everything went well for the first half of the day but the trial had to be stopped shortly after lunch when a submarine contact was identified approaching the area at eight knots. A brief message on underwater telephone established that *Tiptoe* was also aware of the intruder. The trial was interrupted while everybody headed off at high speed to a new area to the west. The trial started again and once again had to be stopped after the first few hours when the irksome intruder inserted itself slowly into the scene.

And so it continued, tempers grew short as plans and programme times were changed again and again. Eventually *Tiptoe* had to leave to take up her next programmed task and the trial was terminated although only about half of the required runs had been completed. The frigate was left to make her own way back towards Devonport. To avoid wasting valuable sea time, opportunities were taken to carry out a series of drills and exercises on the way home. While this was going on the sonar crew were getting plenty of practice because the snooping submarine had now moved to within a few miles of the frigate and was not hiding his presence.

The Captain decided at this point to try to turn the tables on the 'Foxtrot' submarine. The frigate began to use active sonar and make a series of runs towards the submarine. Conventionally powered submarines have one significant disadvantage in that they must come to the surface every few days to recharge their batteries, change the foetid air inside the boat and perhaps get rid of accumulated rubbish. For the Soviet submariner there was one more potential problem. They were not allowed to operate on the surface or 'snort' within sight of NATO vessels.

The sea and weather conditions in our part of the South Western Approaches were unusually benign. The sea was calm and blue, reflecting clear blue autumn skies and making sonar conditions easier for the surface hunter.

We knew that the submarine had been submerged for at least seven days and he would be getting anxious to get to the surface and at least to start charging his batteries and clearing his air by snorting. We were able to identify the submarine approaching the surface and every time he did so we would manoeuvre the ship to get right in his way, as though we were blissfully unaware of his presence and intentions. Life started to become frustrating for the submariner.

This 'cat and mouse' procedure continued for a couple of days by which time the submarine's underwater speed had been reduced to a crawl. Eventually he decided to stop, allow the boat to sink to the sea-bed at a depth of just over three hundred feet and wait us out. The frigate stopped and waited on the surface above the submarine still pinging away on active sonar. The noise of the sonar transmissions bouncing off the hull of the submarine would have added to the discomfort of those inside.

Time passed and after waiting stationary for six hours the submarine released a cloud of accumulated rubbish, presumably through one of the torpedo tubes.

The wait continued.

As the sun eased down towards the western horizon a new development occurred. The passive sonar, listening quietly above the submarine, picked up a popping noise. At first it was thought to be another attempt to discharge rubbish from the submarine but less than a minute later a startled yell came from the lookout on the bridge. Ignoring the proper form of report he shouted "Look at that!" at the same time pointing towards a position beyond the starboard beam. There, bobbing on the surface was a blue cylindrical object, with a thin metal aerial in the process of unfolding itself. It was a Soviet submarine communications buoy.

The First Lieutenant was among the many crew members on the upper deck, taking advantage of the late afternoon sunshine.

"Away Searider!" he roared. The starboard side, Atlantic Searider rigid inflatable boat was already rigged and suspended from its launching crane. Within seconds it was in the water and a few moments later the big fifty-five horsepower outboard was running and the boat was racing away from the ship's side heading purposely towards the communications buoy which was still bobbing on the surface of the water.

The First Lieutenant could see the lanky figure of the ship's Leading Physical Trainer, leaning far out over the bow of the speeding Searider, clutching a business-like set of bolt croppers in his two hands.

The Searider started to decelerate as it approached within a few feet of the buoy; the bolt croppers reached out within inches of the plastic covered cable attached to the buoy and the jaws slammed shut. Half a second beforehand the buoy disappeared. The jaws of the bolt cropper closed on air.

The hunt was over. The chastened submarine was allowed to slither away, mission unaccomplished and the frigate set off back to Devonport.

****

Sixty miles away, in an old, traditional, village pub on the eastern edge of Dartmoor a small group of acquaintances was assembled in a secluded booth with a wooden table between them. Three men and one woman were enjoying their evening. The last of several bundles of used notes were disappearing into pockets and a handbag while the smartest and tallest member of the group was just completing an unctuous set of congratulations addressed to his companions.

"And there's plenty more where that came from," he said, as glasses were raised and drained once more. "We know how to be generous."

The light darkened in the booth as a shadow fell across the table. Two men, dressed almost identically in blue pinstripe suits stood at the entrance to the booth. The shorter man stretched his hand forward, holding an official looking card where all the drinkers could see it.

"You are under arrest," he said quietly, "and you will be charged with contravention of the Official Secrets Act. Espionage, I think we call it." Other men stepped forward including two uniformed police officers and the four spies were hustled outside into waiting cars.

A hundred miles further east, on the A27 between Portsmouth and Southampton, a smart new Volvo estate car was overtaken by an unmarked police car and forced into the side of the road. Three men in plain clothes leapt from the police car and surrounded the Volvo. One of the men pointed a hand gun at the driver. "Out of the car!" he shouted. "Put your hands up!"

The driver of the Volvo was shaking as he climbed out. He was a slightly built man in his mid-forties dressed in the uniform of a Royal Naval sub-lieutenant. He was on his way home to Southampton to surprise his wife with the brand new car. He had come from the Admiralty Underwater Weapons Establishment on Portsdown Hill, where he was an expert in the recently developed passive sonar equipment.

Dimly he heard the man with the gun say "You are under arrest for activities in contravention of the Official Secrets Act."

Out to Lunch

We were a small and happy bunch. Two operational boats, representing all that was left of the once mighty Coastal Forces Command. Each boat was manned by just seventeen ratings and three officers and we all talked, behaved and dressed differently to the rest of the navy. We were, in some ways a throwback to the boats which once ruled the roost in the Channel.

Among the officers I was the "third hand". That meant that as a newly promoted sub-lieutenant, I was responsible for the navigation of the boat and for the tedious task of ensuring that all of the hundreds of charts we held – most of which would never be used – were kept up to date. In this I had the occasional assistance of the Navigator's Yeoman but he was also one of the seamen and he had other calls on his time.

The really exciting aspect of being part of what our Commanding Officer was pleased to call "The First Fast Patrol Boat and Coastal Forces Squadron" was that we sailed in the fastest warships in the world. We could also perform every role that previously, individual specialised coastal forces vessels had been built to undertake.

Powered by three Bristol Proteus gas turbines with a further two Rover gas turbines providing domestic power, we could reach fifty-six knots and we could cruise easily at fifty-three knots in sea states up to force seven. We were armed with a selection of weapons which included four torpedoes, two Bofors guns, four heavy machine guns, twelve mines and six disposable additional fuel tanks. Obviously we couldn't carry all of these at the same time but we could liberally mix-and-match and we could role change very quickly without outside help. Typically, we might rig as a torpedo boat with one deck gun, or turn ourselves into a gunboat with both Bofors and an array of machine guns. As a very fast minelayer we could lay up to twelve mines per session and use our speed to get to and from the minefield before anyone knew we were around. We could also travel very long distances using the extra tanks and then perhaps creep inshore to land clandestine groups.

Launching a torpedo attack was particular fun. We were not fitted with conventional torpedo tubes. Instead we launched the "fish" by simply releasing them from their deck securing points and allowing them to roll over the side. As soon as the torpedoes hit the water we would throttle back to forty knots so that we would not overtake the torpedoes, which travelling at forty-five knots would be much slower than the boat. As soon as the torpedoes were on their way we would slam back up to over fifty knots while releasing a thick smoke screen to cover our retreat.

And of course, cruising at fifty-three knots, we could be back in harbour quite quickly.

We were commanded and led by one of the most charismatic men in the navy. A lieutenant commander, he had spent the entire Second World War in Coastal Forces. He had served in every type of boat on every kind of mission and had borne a charmed existence, despite having several boats shot to pieces, blown up or sunk under him. He wore a chest-full of medals which included one Distinguished Service Cross and two DSOs – among many others. He wore his battered uniform cap, always with a gleaming white cover, at a disapproved jaunty angle, was routinely seen strolling about the base in a white roll-neck sweater and sea-boots and was given regularly to addressing Admirals and other senior worthies by their Christian names, or even nick-names.

Apart from a few set-piece exercises he did pretty well what he liked with the two boats under his command and he paid scant regard to the rules on landing alcohol and cigarettes.

He was a raconteur, a fount of knowledge and a superb seaman and ship-handler. There were never any defaulters on these two boats and if any minor crimes came to light, our

Captain dealt with them in his own ingenious way. The 'lads' thought of him as some kind of Sea-God who, they believed, could do no wrong.

One evening in the early summer, the Skipper announced to his officers that we would be going to Guernsey for lunch. This meant a return trip of perhaps two hundred and twenty nautical miles, say two and a half hours each way, from our base in *HMS Dolphin*, the south coast submarine headquarters. It also meant that although we would all be going to Guernsey, only the Skipper would be going to lunch

At eight-thirty the next morning we cast off our lines and rumbled gently away from the jetty. We rounded Fort Blockhouse at fifteen knots and were doing over forty as we roared past Gilkicker Point heading for the Nab Tower. An hour and a half later we were nosing our way into the harbour of St Peterport to tie up alongside White Rock Pier.

The tides in the Channel Islands run through a very considerable range. The height between high and low water of a spring tide can be over thirty feet and we were arriving at the top of a spring tide. The boat was secured alongside the ancient stone pier, the Skipper came out of his small cabin looking spruced up and wearing his battered cap at an even more jaunty angle than usual. He hopped ashore and disappeared along the pier. The hands went off for their daily issue of grog, supervised by me and then we all settled down to a light, and generally tinned, lunch in the various messes.

We had been told that the Skipper's lunch would take about two hours, so an hour and a half after our arrival we started the engines and singled up the lines, ready for a swift departure. This was at about two o'clock. At half past two the engines were shut down again to allow them to cool. The hands were stood down. There was no sign of the Skipper. By three o'clock the First Lieutenant was looking really worried. He was the one who would get it in the neck if we failed to arrive before the civilian dockside riggers at the base finished work for the day.

At a quarter past three we looked up towards the top of the stone pier, and there, in the distance we could discern a group of people making their way slowly towards us. The tide had dropped considerably since our arrival and the top of the pier was now at least twenty feet above the deck of the boat, so it was difficult to make out who was in the group advancing along the pier above us.

The First Lieutenant called the hands to 'harbour stations' and ordered the engines to be started once more. At this point the group on the pier had arrived at the start of a set of stairs set into the side of the pier. They started gingerly down the slippery steps and I could see at last why they were moving so slowly and carefully. They were carrying something between them.

"Single up!" ordered the First Lieutenant and several ropes came snaking back to the fore and after decks. I checked that all was well aft and then made my way to the bridge. The group on the steps had almost reached the level of the boat and I saw that what they were carrying was a body. The body was that of our Skipper! His limbs were loose and flopping about. He had a stupid-looking lopsided grin on his face and he seemed to be muttering something to his companions. He had obviously enjoyed a very good "lunch" and was now as drunk as a lord.

The Skipper's friends came aboard and dumped him in the wardroom, before reassembling on the stone stairway beside the boat.

"Let go aft, let go for'ard!" The last of the mooring lines came aboard and the First Lieutenant appeared beside me on the bridge. He moved to the steering console and, taking bridge control of the engines, he started to manoeuvre the boat away from the jetty. Once clear, the boat reversed around a half-circle, paused, and then started to move ahead.

We cleared Guernsey Harbour pretty quickly and then turned north to weave our way through the initial hazards towards Alderney. We had two and a half hours to get back to Portsmouth before the riggers started either 'knocking-off' or thinking about overtime. I worked out that in the benign sea conditions and with a bit of tide behind us we would arrive with ten or fifteen minutes to spare. The First Lieutenant started to look happier.

Once we had passed through the Alderney Race – in fairly spectacular fashion at fifty-two knots – the First Lieutenant went down to the wardroom to try to get the Skipper sufficiently sober to avoid attracting undue attention on our arrival back in *HMS Dolphin*, and I carried on driving the speeding ship.

About half an hour later, by which time Cherbourg and the Cotentin Peninsular were both disappearing astern I had settled down on a steady course at fifty knots, steering to pass close to the south of St Catherine's Point on the Isle of Wight. The only other person on the bridge was the helmsman who combined his duties with those of signalman and lookout.

The air was warm, the sea was almost calm and the sun was shining. With the wind in my hair and the boat bounding along like an unfettered panther, it was exhilarating.

Then I heard a voice at my elbow. We were not alone! "This is great, isn't it?" said the voice, echoing my own thoughts of a few moments before.

I looked to my left and saw a man standing on the lower step leading into the bridge. He was wearing a belted brown raincoat and clutching a trilby hat. I had never seen him before! "Yes" I said, weakly, in answer to his rhetorical question.

I was about to ask the man who he was and where he had come from when another one appeared, similarly clothed. "Gee," he said. "This is great, really great."

I stood there dumbfounded, then the first visitor asked "By the way, when do we get back to Guernsey?"

"We're not going back to Guernsey, we're going to Portsmouth, I mean Gosport, that is," I replied.

Both faces fell. "But we've got to get back" said the first visitor, rather plaintively.

"Yes" said his companion, "I left my shop open."

"And mine. I thought we'd only be a short while." He looked as if he was about to weep.

"What sort of shops are they," I said, trying to be helpful, as the boat thundered along, leaving a long straight wake pointing generally back in the direction of the islands.

"I'm a wine merchant," said number one, looking devastated.

"Mine's an off-license. Can we really not go back?" begged number two.

I started to explain the deadlines we were working to when I was interrupted by the arrival of the First Lieutenant. He was quickly and earnestly made aware of the problem by our visitors and he led them away, presumably to ply them with a gin or two to drown their sorrows.

****

The last I saw of our two unfortunate visitors was as they climbed into a taxi heading towards the small airport that existed in Portsmouth at that time. They were hoping to hire a light aircraft – not a cheap exercise – to get them home to rescue what might be left of their vulnerable businesses.

The End